HOW THEY MET,
AND OTHER STORIES

david levithan

ALFRED A. KNOPF

NEW YORK

Copyright © 2008 by David Levithan

All rights reserved. Published in the United States by Alfred A. Knopf, an imprint of Random House Children's Books, a division of Random House, Inc., New York. Originally published in hardcover in the United States by Alfred A. Knopf in 2008.

Knopf, Borzoi Books, and the colophon are registered trademarks of Random House, Inc.

Some of the stories contained in this work were originally published as follows:

"The Alumni Interview" in *Sixteen: Stories About That Sweet and Bitter Birthday*, edited by Megan McCafferty (Three Rivers Press, an imprint of the Crown Publishing Group, a division of Random House, Inc., 2004)

"Lost Sometimes" in *21 Proms*, edited by David Levithan and Daniel Ehrenhaft (Scholastic, Inc., 2007)

"Princes" in *Every Man for Himself: Ten Original Stories About Being a Guy*, edited by Nancy Mercado (Dial Books, a member of Penguin Group [USA] Inc., 2005)

"Breaking and Entering" in *Rush Hour: Reckless*, edited by Michael Cart (Delacorte Press, an imprint of Random House Children's Books, a division of Random House, Inc., 2006)

"What a Song Can Do" in *What a Song Can Do: 12 Riffs on the Power of Music*, edited by Jennifer Armstrong (Alfred A. Knopf, an imprint of Random House Children's Books, a division of Random House, Inc., 2004)

Visit us on the Web! www.randomhouse.com/teens

Educators and librarians, for a variety of teaching tools, visit us at www.randomhouse.com/teachers

The Library of Congress has cataloged the hardcover edition of this work as follows:
Levithan, David.
How they met, and other stories / David Levithan.
p.   cm.
Summary: A collection of eighteen stories describing the surprises, sacrifices, doubts, pain, and joy of falling in love.
ISBN 978-0-375-84886-5 (trade) — ISBN 978-0-375-94886-2 (lib. bdg.) —
ISBN 978-0-375-84942-8 (e-book)
1. Love stories, American. 2. Short stories, American. [1. Love—Fiction. 2. Short stories.] I. Title.
PZ7.L5798Ho 2008
[Fic]—dc22
2007010586

ISBN 978-0-375-84323-5 (tr. pbk.)

Printed in the United States of America
December 2009
10 9 8 7 6 5 4 3 2

First Trade Paperback Edition

For Nancy

(The book of love would not be long and boring
were she the editor)

AUTHOR'S NOTE

This book starts, bizarrely enough, with me in physics class.

It was my junior year of high school. Despite the best efforts of my physics teacher, I was continually bored out of my wits. I needed something to do besides pay attention, and passing notes to my friend Lynda only occupied about half the time. So I decided to write a story, going through the physics book (it would look like I was being studious!) and finding as many romantic notions as possible within its pages (I would not be studious at all!). I think I started in November, and by February I had finished the story. I decided to give it to my friends for Valentine's Day. The next year, they wanted another. And so on, for all the years after.

Not all of these stories are official valentine stories—I can, it seems, write about love and its follies year-round. But when putting together this book of stories about love ("love stories" has the wrong feel to it—I prefer "stories about love"), I decided to go all the way back. As a result, this book contains that first valentine story ("A Romantic Inclination") and the one that came the year after ("Memory Dance," which is still my mom's favorite). Instead of trying to rewrite them as I'd write them now, I've decided to leave them as I wrote them in high school, give or take some punctuation and an awkward last line. "The escalator, a love story" (from college), "Intersection," "The Number of People Who Meet on Airplanes," "Flirting with Waiters," "Starbucks Boy," and "Miss Lucy Had a Steamboat" were also valentine stories, as were "The Good Witch," "Andrew Chang," "Lost Sometimes," and "Skipping the Prom," a medley of prom riffs that I turned into separate stories here. (My novels *Boy Meets Boy*, *The Realm of Possibility*, and *Are We There Yet?* also started as valentine stories.)

All of the stories in this book (indeed, most of the stories I've written) have been proofread by friends of mine. It is foolish to try to list them all, and I'm sure I'm going to overlook some of them, but I'd like to attempt to thank them for taking the time and helping to make me the writer I am. So thanks to the proofreaders, the suggestion-makers, and the story-encouragers (in order of appearance): Mom and Dad, Adam, Mayling Birney, Lynda Hong, Jennifer Bodner, Eliza Sporn, Jennifer Fain, Cary Retlin, Michael Rothman, Andrew Farmer, Piper Hoffman, Shira Epstein, Jennifer Corn, Alistair Newbern, Karen Popernik, David Leventhal, Joanna Fried, Janet Vultee, Ellen Miles (I think all the pages are here this time), Nancy Mercado, Dan Poblocki, Nancy Hinkel, Brian Selznick, Billy Merrell, Nick Eliopulos, and Allison Wortche, as well as my friends (past and present, authorial and editorial) at Scholastic, my friends at Random House, my Teen Author Drinks Night cohorts, and the fine purveyors of Pink Drinks.

These stories aren't interconnected . . . but of course they are, in a way. They don't share characters, but they share many other things. I'm sure I don't even recognize all of the connections now. I know people are afraid of story collections—they don't get the same respect as novels—but I don't understand why. Together, these stories say much more than they would apart. *How They Met* refers not only to the characters in the stories but also to the stories themselves. Here they are, meeting for the first time. In the same way that paragraphs meet, and sentences meet, and words meet.

Enjoy the intersections.

—D.L.

CONTENTS

STARBUCKS BOY

It was my aunt who pimped me out.

We had this arrangement: I would get to live with her for a few weeks over the summer and take a pre-college course at Columbia before my senior year. In return, I wouldn't have to do a thing besides stay out of the way. It sounded like a good plan to me, except that when I got to Columbia on the first day of summer classes, I found that my course had been dropped. Apparently, there'd been a notice that nobody in my family had bothered to notice.

I thought Aunt Celia would be mad. Or at least concerned. But instead she said, "Well, this could actually solve Elise's problem."

Elise was a friend of Aunt Celia's who lived in the same apartment building. She had a six-year-old daughter.

"I'm sure you're wonderful with children," Aunt Celia told me.

This was an especially strange statement coming from Aunt Celia, who (as far as I could tell) considered the continued existence of children to be something akin to a plague. We have a picture we love to look at in my immediate family, taken right after my brother, Jonathan, was born. It's Aunt Celia's turn to hold him, and from the look on her face and the positioning of her body, you'd think that someone had asked her to cradle a ten-pound turd. Nothing personal against Jonathan—I'm sure she was the same with me. As Jonathan and I grew up, Aunt Celia always gave us presents to "save for later." For my seventh birthday I received a pair of Tiffany candlesticks. For my eighth, it was a matching finger bowl. I freaked out, thinking a finger bowl was meant to hold fingers. (Aunt Celia left the room so my parents could explain.) When I turned thirteen, Aunt Celia actually seemed relieved. She finally stopped maintaining any pretense of treating me like a child, and started treating me like a lesser form of adult instead.

"Aren't you?" she now prompted. "Wonderful? With children?"

I didn't know where we were going with this, but I was sure that if I had no reason to stay in New York, Aunt Celia would ship me back to suburbia faster than she could dial out for dinner. Even if I found a way to avoid being underfoot, she would be unnerved by the *concept* of me being underfoot.

"I'm wonderful with children," I assured her. Various instances of me "babysitting" Jonathan flashed through my head—we hadn't been allowed to have pets, so I'd often encouraged him to act like one. I thought it best not to mention the particulars of my sitting experience, which, at its most extreme, stopped just short of accidental lobotomy.

"Perfect," she said. Then she picked up her cell phone off the front table, speed-dialed, and told the person on the other end, "Elise, it's Celia. I have a solution for the whole Astrid affair. My nephew . . . yes, Gabriel. The one I was telling you about . . . escaping my sister, yes. Well, it seems that his course has been canceled. And I happen to know he's wonderful with children. A complete charmer. . . . Yes, he's entirely free. . . . I'm sure those hours would be fine. . . . He's delighted. . . . You'll see him then. . . . Yes, it's quite a loaded potato. . . . Absolutely my pleasure!"

She hung up and looked at me like I'd just been checked off a list.

"It's all set," she said. "Although you'll have to dress nicer than that."

"What's all set?" I asked. If I couldn't do it in a T-shirt, I was worried.

"Why, your job. For the next three weeks."

"Which is . . . ?" I coaxed.

She sighed. "To take care of Elise's daughter, Arabella. You'll love her. She's *wonderful*."

No follow-up questions were possible. With an air kiss and a trail of perfume, Aunt Celia was off.

I started the next morning at eight. My class was supposed to have started at ten, and I'd looked forward to the extra hours of sleep. Instead, Aunt Celia came into my room at seven-fifteen, turned on the lights, released a low-octaved "Be ready by eight," and left before I could see her without the compensations of makeup.

Even after I cured my early-morning dayblindness with two cups of coffee and a shower prolonged by ten minutes of tangential thinking, I still wasn't fully awake when I rang the doorbell of apartment 8C. I looked presentable enough in my button-down shirt and khakis, but my mind felt buttoned-down and khaki as well. I was already starting to resent my new job.

Aunt Celia's friend Elise was three-quarters out the door when she opened it for me.

"You must be Gabriel," she said. "I've heard so much about you. Come in."

Elise was one of those women who exercised so often that she was starting to look like a piece of exercise equipment herself. She walked around the apartment as if she were still on a treadmill, telling me about emergency numbers and people to call and when to expect her back.

"I really appreciate you doing this," she said, putting on her jacket and leading me down a hallway. "Arabella's back here."

Arabella's door was decorated with a framed copy of the unicorn tapestry from The Cloisters. Elise knocked three quick raps into the door, then opened it for me. I was astounded, but not particularly surprised, by the room that was revealed to me. It was everything you might expect from a fairly rich New York City girl named Arabella. It was designed like a *Vogue* version of Disney, with a four-poster bed and no-poster walls. Pink was the dominant color, with blue and green playing the major supporting roles. My attention was caught by a number of wide-eyed dolls relegated to size-order rows on a magisterial display shelf, as if they were about to take a class picture and had dressed for the occasion. This was the room I had never dreamed about as a little boy, and still feared now.

Even though the light in the room was on, Arabella remained under the covers, reading by flashlight. I could see the beam breaking through the comforter, and could hear the pages turn even as her mother called her name. Finally, as the calling grew more insistent, Arabella emerged. She was not, as I'd expected, sleek and steely like her mother. In fact, she was pudgy and flushed, her hair only making a halfhearted effort at curling. Her expression was sour, her clothing dour, and her anger at being interrupted was palpable. She held up her Berenstain Bears book and said, *"I'm trying to read!"*

Elise took it in stride.

"Well, I'm heading off, Arabella. Gabriel will take care of you until Manolo comes at two. *Comprenez-vous?*"

"Oui."

Arabella didn't seem to pay me any mind, and once her mother left the apartment, I remained standing there awkwardly. Arabella didn't return under her covers, but she continued to use the flashlight over every page.

Stupidly, I hadn't brought any reading material of my own. So I reached for a copy of *Pete's a Pizza*, only to be chastised when I picked it up.

"You should ask first," Arabella said.

I apologized.

"I don't go out until ten," she told me. "You can watch TV if you want."

"Do you mind if I read some of these instead?" I asked, gesturing to her bookshelf.

"Sure," she replied. "Just don't say them out loud."

I started with a few picture books, then found a copy of *Charlie and the Chocolate Factory* and began to read that. Every now and then I'd look up and check on my babysittee. I could see her concentrating on each word of every page; only after a sentence was through would she look at the pictures. It was cool to see reading become such a transparent act—it was as if her face had a different expression for each punctuation mark, and when there was dialogue you could see her actually listening to it in her head. One time she caught me watching her and grimaced. I quickly returned to my own book, and didn't smile or even acknowledge it when she started to take books from the pile that I'd already read.

At precisely ten o'clock, Arabella announced, "It's time to go."

Elise hadn't said anything about whether or not we could leave the building, but I assumed it was okay. Arabella swiftly moved to the front door, undoing the locks and bolts as if they were pieces of an ancient Chinese puzzle. She pointed out the spare keys and then instructed me how to lock up once the door was closed again.

I had always secretly suspected that rich New York City kids acted twice as old as they really were. The three-year-olds acted six, the six-year-olds acted twelve, the twelve-year-olds partied like they were twenty-four, and each eighteen-year-old took on a thirty-six-year-old's weariness. Because they had seen the city, they felt they'd seen the world. Whereas those of us in the suburbs had simply seen the suburbs.

I will admit: I was still somewhat amazed and intimidated by New York City and its complex hugeness. Back home when I wanted to go somewhere, I jumped in my car and drove there. But the city required the higher math of navigation, factoring in subway grids and bus paths and street maps, so many letters and numbers and names and letter-number combinations and number-name combinations. The basic act of considering a local distance in terms of east, west, north, and south was bizarre to me; those words, I felt, should be used to describe coasts or countries, not a place two blocks over and one block up.

Arabella didn't seem fazed. Even though she was barely taller than the hydrants, she knew exactly where she was going. Since we were near Central Park, I thought we might be heading for the zoo, or a museum, or a playground. It was a perfect July day— sunny, but with the feeling that God had left the windows open.

At the end of the first block, Arabella waited, even though there was a walk sign. I didn't understand, so after a moment she said to me, a little impatiently, "You need to hold my hand when we cross the street."

Such a strange thing, to hold a six-year-old's hand. Especially a six-year-old you've only just met. A toddler will grab hold of your finger, and someone your own age will clasp on to your whole hand, but with six-year-olds it's something in between, this acknowledgment that they can't be the one to take hold, so you have to do all the holding, folding your hand around theirs, feeling so much bigger and responsible. It's weird and it's scary and it's nice. Neither Arabella nor I said a word, and as soon as we got back to the curb, she pulled away and I let go until the next curb.

"Where are you taking me?" I asked.

"I want to try a new Starbucks," she replied.

"Are you sure you're allowed to go to Starbucks?"

"I go there *all the time*."

Elise had told me to call if there was an emergency, but I figured the prospect of undue caffeination didn't really count as one. In fact, Arabella made it seem like going to Starbucks was the most natural thing in the world, so I followed along. We only had to walk five blocks to hit the nearest one. It was now ten-fifteen, and the morning rush was over. Instead the seats were filled by the daytrippers, the patrons for whom the word *ensconced* was no doubt termed. Laptops were open, bookmarks were orphaned on tables, and newspapers were set out to be read section by section. An idle idyll. Suddenly I felt more at home.

And then I looked behind the counter.

Now, it has to be one of Starbucks's more brilliant marketing strategies to maintain at least one completely dreamy guy behind the counter at any given shift. This guy is invariably known as

Starbucks Boy to the hundreds of regular customers who have a crush on him, and the glory of it is that he always seems just accessible enough to be within reach, but never accessible enough to actually touch. Starbucks Boy wears short sleeves even in the winter, so you can study his arms when you're feeling too shy to stare at his face (in hopes of catching an eye sparkle or a dimple). Depending on the location of the Starbucks, you can imagine that the minute he gets off work, he heads off to rehearse some new songs with his band, or surf the big waves, or shoot an indie film. He is, unlike most beautiful people you've ever encountered, friendly—and you honestly believe it's not because that's a part of his job. He banters with the counter girls relentlessly, whether it's cornrowed Latisha, corn-fed Barbara, or corn-toed Betty. You listen in on their in-jokes, and then think that the way he says "Good morning" or "Have a good one" or "Here you go" to you is a little different from the way he says it to anyone else. Or at least that's the hope.

The dreamy guy at this Starbucks wasn't working the counter. Instead he was working a broom behind it, smiling as he swept. At first I didn't get the smile, but then I realized he was listening to the radio, to Norah Jones sliding her voice around the notes. In his own way, he was dancing along.

I was so busy not-looking-but-looking that I didn't notice Arabella arrive at the front of the line.

"Can I help you?" the counter girl asked. She was about my age, with her hair pulled into a ponytail and her face pulled into a ponyfront.

Suddenly, Arabella became shy. She leaned into me and whispered, "I want a vanilla mocha decaf latte but with no mocha."

I figured the counter girl had heard, but instead of punching it in, she stared at me. So I said, "She'd like a vanilla mocha decaf latte, hold the mocha."

"You mean like a vanilla steamer?" the bored barista asked.

"No!" Arabella shouted. "I want a vanilla mocha decaf latte, *hold the mocha!*"

"One vanilla mocha decaf latte, hold the mocha," the bore-ista repeated.

Arabella pulled on my shirt. I leaned down and she whispered, "I have my purple cup." She rummaged through the small Hello Kitty purse she'd brought and pulled it out.

I could sense a stop to the sweeping, and could imagine Starbucks Boy finally noticing me as I said to the counter girl, "And would you mind putting it in this purple cup?"

"I'm sorry, we can only refill Starbucks mugs," she said.

I looked down to Arabella and saw she was on the verge of an outburst.

"C'mon," I said.

The barista looked offended by this plea—I was violating the Starbucks Code of Customer Behavior. But she would be violating the Starbucks Code of Employee Behavior to tell me to piss off, so we were at a standstill.

Arabella chimed in with a "Pleeeeeeeeease," and that's what did it. Starbucks Boy leaned in, took the cup out of my hand, and said, "No problem."

Then he smiled. At me. The kind of smile that feels like there's a wink attached to it.

I ordered an iced chai, then paid with my hard-earned (well, unearned parental) dollars. Arabella and I shifted over to the pickup counter, where Starbucks Boy was already waiting with her vanilla milk. Frustratingly, a Starbucks Boy never wears a name tag, so you just have to imagine his name is Dalton or Troy or Dylan. As my Starbucks Boy handed Arabella her drink, I observed that he gave her the same smile he gave me. I realized how stupid I was being, thinking his attentions were anything more than routine. Then, when he handed over my drink and our hands accidentally touched, I forgot that realization entirely.

Arabella picked out one of the superlong straws to sip her milk with, and I drank the minute's worth of liquid that had been given to me with an afternoon's worth of ice cubes. When we were finished, I stole one last glance at Starbucks Boy, who was making some foam. I almost went up and purchased a mini bundt cake just to get another view, then I dismissed myself as too silly for words (this was a full conversation in my head) and ushered Arabella (who'd lost interest in her drink after six carefully spaced sips) outside. I proposed a stop at the Central Park Zoo, and she acted like she was humoring me by saying yes.

I found myself wanting to impress her, like we were on a date. I rattled off facts about polar bears and penguins, and was excited when she seemed mildly interested. She started asking me the names of each of the animals—not their scientific names, but their proper names, like Freezy or Gertrude. I gave her the answers, making them up as we went along, and it took a good dozen species before Arabella figured out I was kidding.

"The emu is not named Clifford," she said. "Clifford is a dog."

"Did I say Clifford?" I backtracked. "I meant Gifford. Like Kathie Lee."

"Who's Kathie Lee?"

"Kathie Lee's the sea otter. Let's go see her."

I had thought it wouldn't be any problem for us to get back by two, and because of that I didn't bother to check the clock on my cell phone. I was shocked when I finally saw that we only had twenty-five minutes to get home.

"You forgot lunch," Arabella said as we headed home.

"You didn't tell me you were hungry," I replied, and then immediately felt the way any adult feels when he or she picks an argument with a six-year-old—namely, stupid.

"I was," Arabella said, and that was that.

We got back with three minutes to spare.

"Don't worry," Arabella told me as I made her a pb & j sandwich in the kitchen. "Manolo's always late."

I nodded and asked her who Manolo was.

"My French tutor," she replied. Then she asked, "Do you have a boyfriend?"

I was about to bitch and moan—the usual response—but then I realized who I was talking to. Only in New York (and maybe San Francisco) could a six-year-old have gaydar.

"How do you know I'm gay?" I asked. I genuinely wanted to know. My wardrobe wasn't infused with pink or rainbows, and I certainly hadn't been very flamboyant in her presence. I wondered what my tells were.

"The way you look at boys," she said. "You're gay."

The doorbell rang. Arabella made no move to answer it.

"I'll get it," I said. It took me a minute to walk to the door, but two minutes to get the locks open.

"The top one first and to the left," the voice on the other side of the door said. "Then the middle one to the right. Then the bottom one, twice around to the left. Now turn the knob."

When I finally got it open, I found a guy a few years older than me, wearing a winter sweater on a summer day. He had Harry Potter glasses and a Beatrix Potter body.

"*Bonjour,*" he said.

" '*Allo,*" I said, trying to sound Cockney but ending up sounding Klingon.

"You must be Astrid's successor," he continued. "I'm charmed to meet you."

"And you must be Manolo," I said. "Or do you prefer Manny?"

At that last word, he shuddered.

"Manolo," he said. "Is *la fille* ready?"

"She's in *le kitchen.*"

"Can you tell her to meet me in the study?"

"My pleasure."

I watched him stroll off without another look in my direction, then poked my head into the kitchen.

"Your Frenchman's here," I said. "I'm going to head home."

Arabella put her sandwich down and said, "That's fine. I won't tell Mom about lunch as long as you remember tomorrow."

I told her she had a deal.

The next day was much the same, only I was wearing better clothes. I had a suspicion that Arabella was a daily-ritual kind of girl, and if I was going to see Starbucks Boy again, it wasn't going to be in khakis and a button-down.

If Elise or Arabella noticed my more casual attire, neither mentioned it. Instead Elise mentioned that Ivan—the math tutor—was coming at three.

Figuring it might mean extra money—and also figuring I had more than a fair grasp of first-grade math—I told Elise, "If you want, I could tutor Arabella. You know, stay later and do it."

Elise stared down her nose at me. She had to angle her head to do it.

"I'm sure you're very intelligent, but we prefer Arabella's tutors to have graduated college."

"Ivy league?" I asked, tongue in cheek.

"Preferred, but not essential," Elise replied, tongue nowhere near cheek. "We had a lovely girl from Smith, but she went away to India with her new lover."

I didn't think it would win me the argument to point out that I wasn't going to be running off with any lovers anytime soon. I made a mental note to teach Arabella some really stupid knock-knock jokes as retribution.

As I'd predicted, we followed the same morning routine: reading in Arabella's room until ten (once again, I didn't bring my own book, but this time it was deliberate—I enjoyed reading hers), then a stroll down to Starbucks. I kept looking at my reflection in windows as we walked there, checking to see if my hair was flat or if my shirt was billowing the wrong way. Arabella was telling me a story about a girl in her kindergarten class who had eaten a crayon and said it tasted like chicken. I tried to follow.

All of my prayers and fears were answered, because Starbucks Boy was working the register when we walked in. There were two people in front of us, and I obsessively paid attention to the way he talked to them—genial, but nothing special. When we got to the front of the line, he smiled a little wider (I was sure of it) and said, without missing a beat, "One iced chai and one vanilla mocha decaf latte, hold the mocha, in a purple cup, right?"

Was I dealing with some kind of Starbucks Savant, or had he thought my order yesterday was worth remembering? Melodramatic as it may sound (and it certainly *felt* melodramatic), I considered that my entire romantic future might hinge on the answer to that question.

The trouble with flirting with someone at a cash register is that your time together is bound to be fleeting. I could hear the people behind me shuffling and preparing to grumble as I fumbled through my wallet for correct change (saving my singles for the tip jar, where they'd be more noticeable). Starbucks Boy conveyed my order and Arabella's cup to the worker b's behind him, then looked at my wallet and said, "It's cool you have a change pocket. I need one of those in my wallet. I *hate* loose change."

If there was something to say next that would parlay our conversation from reportage to repartee, I couldn't figure it out. So instead of something inspiringly witty, I said, "I got it at H&M. I like it a lot."

"Homosexual and Metrosexual," Starbucks Boy replied. Then, as I thought *WHA?!*, he added, "H&M. I know it stands for something Swedish, but really it should be Homosexual & Metrosexual."

"Yeah," I said. "Mmm-hmm."

"It's a cool wallet."

"Thanks."

Because I'd paid in exact change, there wasn't anything for him to give me back but the receipt. And once he handed that over, I couldn't continue to hold up the line. I didn't think the woman behind me would understand if I turned to her and said, "I just need another moment—I'm admiring his eyes." Or maybe she would, and she'd get further with him than I could.

Homosexual or metrosexual? Or just a fan of mass-produced Swedish fashion?

I hadn't even realized that Arabella had disappeared from my side, which I imagined wasn't the best babysitter behavior on my part. Luckily she was only a few steps away, at the pickup counter.

"He's nice," she observed. I restrained myself from grabbing her by the shoulders and asking, *What else did you notice? Do you think he's into guys? And into me, specifically?* I wished I were back home, where I could send my girl posse in to suss him out.

That afternoon, after I'd abandoned Arabella to Ivan (who looked like the love child of Lenin and Stalin), I found myself ambling by the Starbucks again. I debated whether or not to go in, to see if Starbucks Boy's shift had ended. Then I started to feel like I was exhibiting Typical Stalker Behavior and decided to stalk wallets at H&M instead.

I knew I was getting perilously close to opening up my History of Stupid Things Done in the Name of Crushes, but the insidious thing about the History was that I always felt each new blank page had the potential to transform it into a different book. One successful gesture, one successful relationship would suddenly turn it into a History of Stupid Things Done in the Name of Crushes That Were All Redeemed in the End. If on page 13 I wrote Justin Timberlake's initials with mine in a heart on my sneakers, only to throw them out the next day when Laura Duke teased me for it, or if on page 98 I set up base camp outside Roger Lin's locker just to see if he'd notice me there, or if on page 154 I entered a milkshake-drinking contest to be able to stand next to Mark Tamlin for fifteen minutes, only to have him puke vanilla chum onto my Skechers . . . well, somehow I felt these pages didn't bear consideration as I headed to page 239 and bought a ten-dollar H&M wallet for a boy because it was the only thing in the world I knew for sure he liked, including me. I didn't buy him the same exact wallet—I made his green to my blue—and I didn't actually believe I'd ever give it to him. But at least it provided me with the illusion of doing something proactive.

That night, Aunt Celia asked me how it was going with Arabella. We were at a trattoria down the street from her apartment, her concession for never cooking me dinner.

"Fine," I said.

Aunt Celia swirled the wine in her glass for a second before drinking it. "She's a very talented girl . . . or so Elise tells me."

"She's very smart," I agreed.

Aunt Celia nodded. "Good." Then she speared an asparagus and we remained in silence until she released her next fleeting criticism.

Pretty much the whole time, I was thinking of Starbucks Boy.

The next morning, I couldn't stop myself from being impatient. Arabella also seemed to be pushing the clock to go faster. Instead of spending time on each book, she sped through them, scowling at the illustrated kittens and puppies as if it were their fault that time couldn't move as fast as she turned the pages.

Finally, a little before ten o'clock, she looked at me thoughtfully and said, "Let's go now."

I had spent about a half hour deciding which T-shirt to wear, which was a sure sign of a crush if ever there was one. I was also carrying two wallets—an empty one in my left pocket, an only-marginally-more-full one in my right.

I didn't even accept the possibility that he might not be there when we arrived. I knew that if I entered the Starbucks and didn't see him, I would impale myself on the nearest coffee stirrer.

My heart missed about a thousand beats when we walked in and discovered the surly girly behind the counter. But then Starbucks Boy emerged from the back room, a stack of cups piled high in his hands. Gently he settled them down next to the mocha machines. I felt all the nervous static in my heart empty into my bloodstream.

As he straightened the cups into neat rows, he looked up and saw me. There was instant recognition, and another one of those smiles. As Arabella and I moved to the front of the line, he relieved his co-worker at the cash register.

"The usual?" he asked.

"Thanks," I said, handing over Arabella's purple cup.

Then he went back and *made them himself*. The glum girl returned to the cash register as if it had all been planned.

I thought about leaving the H&M wallet in the tip jar. Then I thought about striking up a conversation and handing it to him. Then I thought about how ridiculous everything was, and all my resolve dissolved. When I picked up Arabella's milk and my chai, my fingers again briefly touched his. But it was just a hand-off, not a hands-on.

"Thanks," I said again.

"My pleasure," he replied. And then we stood there for a second, before I felt goofy and turned away to get a table.

Arabella didn't seem happy with me.

"He's really nice," she said once more, this time between sips.

"He sure is," I agreed, perhaps too enthusiastically.

After about four more sips, Arabella announced she had to go to the girls' room.

I looked at the restroom door and saw I'd need to get the key.

"Are you sure you can't wait until we get home?" I asked.

"I need to go *now*."

"Okay, okay," I mumbled. Then I went back up to the counter. Of course, Starbucks Boy was the one who came to my aid.

"The bathroom key?" I said. He reached over and gave me a key with a plank the size of a gym teacher's clipboard attached.

I felt silly, so I told him, "It's not for me."

He smiled and said, "It would be okay if it was."

Now I felt truly foolish, and knew there was no transition in the universe that could take me to "Hey, I have a wallet for you!" So I took the plank-key and led Arabella to the bathroom.

"Give me the key," she said.

I handed it over, and she locked herself in the bathroom. I decided to guard the door, just in case.

Minutes passed. I finished my chai and threw out the cup. A line started to form for the restroom.

"You okay in there?" I asked through the door.

"It's coming out!" Arabella called back.

More minutes passed.

"How're you doing?"

"Good."

The line grew longer.

I didn't hear any activity inside, and felt like a perv for listening.

The people in the line were getting grumpy. One lady went and got Starbucks Boy.

"How's it going?" he asked.

"Great," I said. "I'm sure she'll just be another second."

Up close, I could not only see his dimples, but also the light stubble on his chin. I so wanted to touch it.

"Arabella?" I called into the bathroom.

"Almost empty!" she shouted back.

Then, even louder, "Oh! There's another!"

Starbucks Boy chuckled.

"How old's your sister?" he asked.

"Oh, she's not my sister."

"She's not?"

"No. I guess I'm . . . uh . . . babysitting."

"I'M HALF EMPTY NOW!" Arabella called out.

Deadpan, as if he hadn't heard it loud and clear, I told him, "She's half empty now."

People were leaving the line, giving up. The lady who'd complained started to complain some more, saying there needed to be a time limit for restrooms, and minors should never, ever be let in on their own. . . .

Starbucks Boy turned on all the charm, and told her there was a bathroom in the Barnes & Noble two blocks away. She only huffed some more, said something about writing Bill Gates to complain, then stomped away.

And it was at that moment—that glorious moment—that the saints went marching in. Because it was at that moment—that wonderful moment—that Starbucks Boy leaned over to me and said, "God, my last boyfriend was *just like that.*"

The tell.

"That must have been fun," I said, my heart break-dancing.

"A blast," he said.

Then he looked down at the door and asked, "Hey, where's the key?"

"Um . . . in there . . . with her."

Starbucks Boy seemed to be torn between amusement and concern. "You know, there isn't another key," he told me.

"No," I said, "I didn't know that." Then I knocked on the door and said Arabella's name again.

"Almost empty!" she called.

Starbucks Boy and I hovered there awkwardly. I could sense he was about to say he needed to get back behind the counter, and I didn't want that to happen. Somehow it made it easier to talk to him when I could see his shoes.

"I'm Gabriel," I said.

He smiled. "I'm Justin."

Justin.

"Three-quarters empty!" Arabella announced.

"It's nice to meet you," I said.

"It's nice to meet you, too."

"I have to wipe now!"

"Okay, Arabella!"

"Is that really her name?"

"Yup."

"I can hear you!"

"Do you live around here?" Starbucks Boy—*Justin*—asked.

"Yeah," I said. Then I added, "For the summer."

"Cool."

Yes yes yes yes yes.

Arabella had fallen silent.

Please may this not be a part of the History . . .

"So, Justin . . ."

"So, Gabriel . . . ?"

I can't believe I'm doing this. I can't believe I'm doing this.

"You wanna—I dunno—get coffee or something sometime?"

Justin smiled. "Not coffee. But yes."

"Not Coffee it is, then."

"Yes, Not Coffee."

As Arabella emerged from the bathroom, hands freshly washed, Justin ran for a pen, then came back with his number on a napkin. Untrusting of napkins, I entered it into my phone.

"Tomorrowish?" Justin asked.

"Sure," I said. "Tomorrowish."

Arabella looked satisfied, but I couldn't tell whether it was from what she'd just done or what I'd just done.

On the way out, she gave me a hint.

"You're going to call him, right?" she asked.

And I said, yes, I was going to call him.

When we got to the first block, she took my hand. And for the rest of the afternoon, she rarely let go.

That night, Aunt Celia got a call from Elise. Aunt Celia's side of the conversation went something like this:

"Hello, Elise. . . . Oh, it was fine. . . . Yes? . . . No! Already? . . . I see. . . . Yes, he's right here. . . . That's really amazing, isn't it? . . . No, I'm sure he won't. . . . I'll make sure he does. . . . No, thank *you*, Elise. Talk later!"

Aunt Celia hung up, then shocked the heavens out of me by saying, "I hear you're going on a date tomorrow."

I still hadn't called Justin—I figured waiting until eight was a good idea, for some arbitrary reason—but I figured that since it *was* going to happen, I could tell her, yes, I had a date tomorrow.

"You know," Aunt Celia said, "Elise told me that Arabella was good, but I had no idea she was *that* good. Three days!"

"What do you mean?" I asked.

"Oh, you're the fourth of Arabella's minders to have been set up by her. It's remarkable, really. Maybe *I* should start taking care of her!"

"She didn't set us up," I said—but immediately I started to wonder. I mean, I was sure I'd had something to do with it. But maybe not everything. . . .

"You're not to quit on Elise, do you understand?" Aunt Celia continued. "The last girl, Astrid, did that. And that other girl—the one who ended up in India with her girlfriend. Poor Elise—she loses sitters faster than I lose umbrellas."

"I won't leave her," I promised.

"And you won't run off to India?"

"Just Starbucks."

Aunt Celia grimaced. "Starbucks is so *crowded*," she judged. "But you do what you want." She gestured toward the take-out menus and told me to order what I wanted for dinner. "I won't be back too late," she told me. "Nor too early, for that matter."

I waited until she was gone before I took out my phone . . . and the green H&M wallet. I imagined myself filling it with lucky pennies and love notes and photobooth strips of Justin and me in playful poses.

"You're such a goofball," I said to myself.

I discarded the notion of waiting until eight and dialed his number. I already had my first line ready.

"You'll never believe this," I'd say. Then I'd tell him the whole story.

Except for the wallet. I wouldn't tell him about the wallet.

I'd save that for an anniversary.

MISS LUCY HAD A STEAMBOAT

The minute I saw Ashley, I thought, *Oh shit. Trouble.*

You have to understand: I grew up in a house where my mother told me on an almost daily basis that until I got married, my pussy was for peeing. In her world, all lesbians talked like Hillary Clinton and looked like Bill, and that included Rosie O'Donnell especially. My mother didn't know any lesbians personally, and she didn't want to know any, either. She was so oblivious that she stayed up nights worrying that I was going to get myself pregnant. There was no way to tell her the only way *that* was going to happen was if God himself knocked me up.

Luckily, I'd learned that the best defense against such hole-headed thinking was to find everything funny. Like the fact that all the sports teams in our school—even the girls' teams—were called the Minutemen. All you had to do was pronounce the first part of that word "my-newt" and it was funny, like suddenly our football team had *Tiny Dicks* written on their jerseys. Or the fact that in the past calendar year, my mother had hit so many mail-boxes, deer, and side mirrors that her license had been suspended. I chose to think she did it on purpose, just so I'd have to drive her around and hear her advice on boys, school, and how bad my hair looked. Hysterical. And, best of all for a quick laugh, there was Lily White—that was her name, swear to God—who certainly enjoyed kissing me in secret. But then when I brought up the idea of, hey, maybe doing it outside of her house, she shut down the whole thing and said to me, "None of this happened."

Well, I knew a punch line when I saw one. So the next day at lunch, when no one was looking, I spilled her Diet Coke all over her fancy shirt and said, "None of this happened." And the next day, my bumper just happened to ram into the side of her daddygirl Cadillac. I left her a note: *None of this happened*. And it didn't happen the next day, either.

I, for one, was amused.

It was hard for me not to feel a little stupid about Lily White. Not because it ended or that it had gone on for three months, but because I'd started it in the first place. Lily was the popularity equivalent of a B-minus student—never the brightest bulb in the room, but still lit. She never laughed at a joke until she saw other people laughing at it, too. Even when we were kissing, she never seemed to admit that we were kissing—it was like I was saying something she couldn't hear, and she was just nodding along to be polite. The first time we got together, it had less to do with romance and more to do with Miller Lite. It took just two cans for her to turn playful. We kissed; it was nice. And for three months we pretty much stuck to that. The kissing was hot, but Lily was pretty insistent about not letting the fire spread. Every time I tried to take her clothes off, she suddenly had somewhere else to be.

Every time I felt her up, she acted like my hands were cold. And every time I tried to go near her pussy, it jumped away.

I could lie and say I swore I was through with girls, but really I figured I needed to find someone better than Lily White. When Ashley Cooper came to town, I was primed.

She made one hell of an entrance.

She was ten minutes late to homeroom, because in her old school homeroom was at 8 and in our school it was at 7:50. Nobody'd told us there was going to be a new girl; they never do.

What I'm saying is: I wasn't expecting her. Then suddenly there was this girl in front of our class, trying to explain to Mr. Partridge who she was, only Mr. Partridge hadn't heard a complete sentence since he was eighty, which was a long time ago. He was telling her she was late, and that he was going to mark her down for being late. She made the mistake of asking him if he even knew who she was, and he shot her a look like she'd just told him that World War II was over. Then he shook his head and said, "Sit down, Antonia."

Man, she looked awesome. Short red hair, full full lips, shirt so tight you could check for tattoos underneath. Most of us put up with Mr. Partridge when we had him for history because at the end of each marking period we could steal his marking book, change the grades, and know we'd be getting A's. But Ashley wasn't the type to let it go. "Who's Antonia?" she asked. "I'm not Antonia."

"Hell you're not," Mr. Partridge chided. "Sit down!"

I thought she'd storm back out; she had that pose. But instead she turned to the class—we were all treating this like gossip unfolding before our eyes—and said, "Who *the fuck* is Antonia?"

I was so snagged. There was no way I could say something to her. But there was no way I could ignore her, either.

"Antonia's my sister," I said.

Ashley walked over to me.

"Do I look like her?" she asked.

"No," I told her—it was really the truth. "But I don't look like her, either, and that's what he calls me all the time."

"So he thinks I'm you?" She didn't sound offended by this, which was a start.

"He's looking forward to the day that a man walks on the moon," I replied. "Don't take it personally."

"I try not to take anything personally, Antonia's Sister."

I had looked at her eyes for a split second, but now I was looking at her arm. The light from the window was hitting it and I couldn't stop staring. I'll admit it—I have a thing for a little hair on a girl's arms. Not head hair or anything like that—just that soft, translucent hair that looks like a spider wove it. She had that, and some freckles, too.

"You're new here," I said. I mean, duh.

"It shows?" she said in a dumb-little-girl voice. She tilted her head to the rest of the class. "Do they always stare like that?"

"I'm not sure they've ever seen a nose ring before. They probably think you're from MTV."

I don't think Ashley was expecting me to joke. Her laugh caught even her by surprise. She kinda laughed like a barking seal. It wasn't very cute, but it was definitely sexy that she didn't care.

"I'm starting to see why Mr. Ancient up there thought I was you."

If she'd asked me to jump her right then and there, I swear I would've. It's like my mind and my body had the same voice, and they were both yelling, *Hell, yeah*. The only difference being that my mind, which knew a little better, added, *Oh shit. Trouble*.

"So do I get your real name?" she asked as the bell rang and we had to head to class.

"Lucy," I told her.

"I'll be seeing you around, Miss Lucy," she said.

That sealed it. I was completely in danger of falling in love.

Nobody'd ever called me Miss Lucy like that before.

Only a certain kind of girl could make *Miss Lucy* sound tough.

There's some history here.

With all due respect to my mother (although I'm not sure how much respect she's truly due), Lucy has never been the right name for me. The role models were all wrong. Like Lucy from the *Peanuts* comics. Okay, so she was probably a lesbian. I mean, her brother's gay (thumbsucker!) and Schroeder, the boy she pretends to have a crush on, is so gay it hurts my teeth. Plus she's friends with Peppermint Patty and Marcie, whose relationship has lasted longer than my grandparents'. But even if she was a lesbian, I wasn't going to be like Lucy. I didn't want to be. You get a sense from watching her that she's going to end up being somebody's evil boss.

And then, of course, there was Lucy Ricardo from *I Love Lucy*. I wanted to love Lucy, really I did. I kept waiting for the episode where Lucy and Ethel finally ran off together and made out. But eventually I realized that wasn't going to happen. Lucy was scatterbrained like me, all right, and I could definitely relate to the way everything she touched turned into a complete mess. But I knew I'd last a whole five minutes with a guy like Ricky. Maybe not even that. I understood that deep down he was supposed to love her and all, but most of the time I found him to be a whining prick. I'd been there—thank you, Lily—and I had no intention to go back again.

That left me with the only famous Lucy remaining: the one who had a steamboat. She came into my life in the same way she comes into most girls' lives—at recess. I was in second grade, and the second-grade girls were sharing the pavement with the fourth-grade girls—the fourth-grade girls being, in my second-grade eyes, girls of infinite wisdom and certitude. I never would have gotten close enough to hear a single word the fourth-grade girls said, but Mrs. Shedlow, the recess supervisor, was a firm believer in democracy, so she'd lined us up second-fourth, second-fourth for the jump-roping. She took one end of the rope and Rachel Cullins's older sister, Eve, took the other. My friend Grace was the first girl to jump, and the rhyme she got was a familiar one:

> Strawberry shortcake
> Cream on top
> Tell me the name
> of your sweet heart.
> Is it A . . . B . . . C . . . ?

Grace's foot hit the rope on B, shackling her in eternal devotion to Barry Lefner for at least the next ten minutes. A fourth-grade girl got to R. But most of the second-grade girls couldn't make it past Evan Eager. I don't know if it was the fact that we were exhausting the alphabetically early boys, or whether it was because Eve knew my name since I was friends with Rachel, but whatever the case, when the rope started turning for me, the strawberry shortcake was sent back to the kitchen, and Miss Lucy sailed right in.

> Miss Lucy had a steamboat
> The steamboat had a bell

Miss Lucy went to heaven
And the steamboat went to

At this point I tripped up in a downward direction, skinning my knee and coming way too close to smudging my favorite shirt. When the next girl went, the shortcake had returned. I walked over to Rachel and asked her who Miss Lucy was.

Now, of all the Cullins sisters, Rachel was always the one to blush fastest. And I'm sure just the mention of Miss Lucy was enough to make her feel like the worst kind of sinner. There was no way she could share the rhyme with me. No decent girl would. My older sister, Antonia, certainly wouldn't. She was already in junior high, planning her hypothetical wedding day.

Luckily, a girl named Heron overheard my question. Heron was fairly new to our school, and generally untested. When Mrs. Park had introduced her to the class, she'd said Heron's name was "Hero . . . with an n." That set Heron back a couple of months. She wore clothes—even then—that seemed like hand-me-downs from when her mother had been in second grade. I didn't know what to make of her.

"C'mere," she said to me now.

Curious, I obliged. She told me to sit down with my legs making a wide V. (Don't worry: I was wearing pants.) Then she sat across from me and touched her feet to mine. She started to make a patty-cake patty-cake motion, and I knew that I was supposed to clap my hands to hers according to a certain order. So far, so good.

"It's like this," she said. And then she presented me with my last possible role model.

Miss Lucy had a steamboat
The steamboat had a bell
Miss Lucy went to heaven
And the steamboat went to
Hello, operator
Please give me number nine
And if you disconnect me,
I will chop off your
Behind the 'frigerator
There was a piece of glass
Miss Lucy sat upon it
And it went right up her
Ask me no more questions
And I'll tell you no more lies
The boys are in the bathroom
Zipping up their
Flies are in the belfry
And bees are in the park
And boys and girls are kissing
In the D-A-R-K
D-A-R-K
D-A-R-K
DARK DARK DARK

It's not a rhyme, because it doesn't rhyme. It's not a song, because there's no real music. It's not a limerick, because it's not Irish. At some point, I guess I just started thinking of it as a biography.

By the time I got to senior year of high school, I figured I'd run Miss Lucy's story through my head at least a thousand times. In the beginning it was a source of endless amusement. Then it was one of my earliest pieces of nostalgia—when I was a sixth grader, I used it to remember the fond innocence of second grade. Then it became a place my mind went from time to time. Science class boring? Well, Miss Lucy had a steamboat. Dying to get off the phone with the friend who won't shut up? Miss Lucy had a steamboat. Stuck in the car while Mom runs in for the dry cleaning? Miss Lucy had a steamboat.

I had no idea what it meant. That was the beauty of it.

I could relate to Miss Lucy because her life made absolutely no sense.

I'd say I was itching to see Ashley again after our first brief conversation, but an itch is something you can scratch, while absence is something you can't really do shit about. She wasn't in any of my classes; since I was in all of the average classes, this meant she was either really smart or really dumb. There was a slim chance she'd just decided this place wasn't for her and had left after homeroom. But that wasn't the option I was hoping for when lunch began.

"You misplace your attention span?" my best friend, Teddy, asked when he caught me looking around.

"There's this new girl," I said.

Teddy snorted. "Now, that didn't take long, did it?"

Teddy was once the new kid, too. He was born in California, but he spent most of elementary school in Korea. Then his parents moved back to California when he was in sixth grade. In tenth grade, they moved again, this time to our town. That's when I met him—the first day of tenth grade. I hated him almost instantly.

His first words to me were "If you're not a [not nice word for lesbian], you sure as hell dress like one."

I must've immediately looked miffed, because he quickly

added, "Hey, to me [not nice word for lesbian] is an affectionate term. After all, I'm a big ol' [rather sexually explicit word for gay man]."

I wasn't ready for terms, affectionate or otherwise, from him. I was still coming to terms with myself, dealing with the anxiety and disappointment and exhilaration of being into girls. I tried avoiding him for months. It didn't work.

"You got it bad, and that ain't good," he said to me now.

"She called me Miss Lucy," I told him.

This made Heron, also at our table, perk up. She'd been reading. She was always reading. She was the only person I knew who'd gotten carpal tunnel syndrome from holding books for too long.

"Miss Lucy is our thing," she said. She wasn't saying it out of jealousy or possessiveness. It was like she wanted to remind herself.

"Where is she?" I asked Teddy. "Use your gaydar."

"You *know* gaydar isn't like air-traffic control," he tsked. "The person actually has to be in the room."

"Well, she's not here," I said. "So I'm going to find her."

"That's ballsy," Teddy said.

I looked to Heron for some help.

"Why not?" she said. That was her version of advice.

As I left the cafeteria, it became a test: If I found her, surely that was a sign that things were meant to be. Granted, the sign wouldn't really spell out what those things were—it would be like a street sign that said STUFF AHEAD. But that was good enough for me.

I found her in the parking lot, leaning on a blue car, eating French fries.

"I had to reward myself for surviving the morning," she explained, offering me some.

"That bad?" I asked, taking a few.

"Yeah, but not without its prospects."

I was so used to being the brazen one that I just about flipped to have someone be brazen in my direction.

"Prospects, eh?" I said, fishing for confirmation.

"Yes, Miss Lucy," she replied, stretching away from the car, toward me. "And I believe the afternoon's already getting better."

You should never kiss someone in the first ten minutes. I know that now, but back then it just seemed like nine minutes too long to wait.

"So, are you girlfriends or what?" Teddy asked me, three weeks after Ashley and I started our thing.

The only place I called her *girlfriend* was in my head. Sometimes I'd say it about a million dozen times in a row, staring at her in class. I wasn't secret about it or anything. Hunger is something you can't hide.

"I dunno," I told him. "I think I'm her girlfriend, and I guess she's mine. We don't talk about it."

"If you're not girlfriends, then what are you?" he pestered.

I didn't tell him the answer, because I was too proud of it and also a little embarrassed by my pride.

Even if I wasn't her girlfriend, I was definitely her Miss Lucy.

"Come over here, Miss Lucy, and give me a hand," she'd say, and I'd be over in a flash, whether it was to sort out her locker, fill in her homework, or unhook her bra.

"I like you, Miss Lucy," she'd tell me, and I'd have to do everything I could not to lob a *love* back at her.

But she could tell. Oh, she could tell.

Lily White could also tell. She could try to hide herself in the cheer squad at lunch or look away when she got near my locker, but damned if the news didn't spread to her ears anyway. I made sure to smile extra wide whenever I saw her. One time, Ashley gave me a big ol' love bite, right under the collar. That day, when I was passing Lily White in the hall, I couldn't help myself. Right when she was looking at me, I pulled the collar down a little to show her.

"That's gross," she said.

"Didn't happen," I told her.

Nobody'd ever bothered to tell me that if you get too caught up in running away from the wolf, you end up in the arms of the bear.

As for Lily White, a few days later she started dating Pete, who was much much nicer than me. But I doubted he was as good a kisser.

"You're a great kisser," Ashley would say.

"Miss Lucy, I'd be lost in this town without you," she'd tell me.

"You're so pretty," she'd swear.

The things she'd do to me, I'd never even had the imagination to imagine.

"When's she going to hang out with us?" Teddy would ask. "Why do the two of you always have to be alone?"

I didn't know how to explain it to him. "It's not that she doesn't like you—" I started.

"How could she? She's never really *met* us."

"She just wants to spend her time with me. Is that so wrong?"

"Yes," Teddy said. "Like this, it is."

Heron didn't say a word.

"I'm through with you," I said. "Can't you think about me for once?"

"You're doing enough of that for all of us," Teddy shot back.

"Forget it. Forget all of it," I said, grabbing my backpack and storming out to the parking lot. I thought I'd find her there, but her car was gone.

"Where are you?" I asked, then felt stupid for doing it.

I didn't go back to the cafeteria. I found my own space, sitting on the floor around the corner from the gym.

I told myself the emptiness I felt was the space I'd hollowed out from missing her. A negative space that was positive. The loss that meant I had something to lose.

I desperately wanted to have something to lose.

Mostly we stayed in places that were public or possibly public— we'd move items from aisle to aisle in Target, trying to come up with the sickest combinations possible, like putting condoms next to the Barbie dolls or hemorrhoid cream with the toothpaste. We'd sneak into crap movies and try to finish the characters' crap lines for them. Then we'd make out in her car and hope nobody came by. We steamed up the windows so much that I could trace hearts in them afterward. Her initials looked good with mine.

My mother couldn't stand it. She needed me to drive her around and listen to her carry on about the sorry state of the world (which stretched about as far as the mall). All I'd told her was that I had a new friend. She said she wanted to meet this new friend. I told her the new friend wasn't a boy, and she got less excited. She had no real advice to give about friendship because she'd never managed to keep a friend in her life. Not that she saw it that way. She felt she had plenty of friends. She just didn't spend any time with them.

I had no intention of introducing her to Ashley, or even of having Ashley in the house. But finally the time came when I wanted us to use a bed. Call me old-fashioned, but I was getting tired of having to do the pleasure thing with a seat belt pressing against my back. Ashley flat-out refused to bring me to her house, so I told her, fine, we'd go to mine. My mother's one great indulgence was getting her hair done, so one afternoon after I dropped her off at the beauty parlor, I sped through a few lights and picked Ashley up to take her home.

"This is such a Miss Lucy bedroom," she said when she saw it.

"What does that mean?" I asked her. For some reason, I didn't think Miss Lucy would have black-painted walls.

"You try so hard not to be frilly," she replied, like she was the queen of frill.

I must've looked a little put out, because she said, "Now, don't be hurt. You can't be hurt, 'cuz I wasn't meaning to hurt you."

She came over and started to cuddle me into her, and it was like my mind stopped having any other thoughts about her besides *now now now*.

I was thirty minutes late picking my mother up.

She took one look at me and said, "What happened to you?"

Ashley, I wanted to tell her. *Ashley's happening to me.*

But instead I told her I'd gotten a flat.

This was a stupid lie.

"Where's the old tire?" she asked when we got home.

"The triple-A guy took it," I told her.

"You're a very bad liar," she said.

"Your hair looks like a camel peed in it," I said back, then stormed to my room and called Ashley to tell her all about it.

"A *camel peed in it?*" Ashley said, laughing.

Suddenly it didn't seem as serious.

"Well, that's what it looked like," I said.

Already the edge was gone. My life could be curvy again, and all it took was a laugh on her end of the phone.

More weeks passed.

I wanted something from her.

I wanted the l-word.

I wanted her to call me her girlfriend.

I wanted to make her cry.

I wanted to know I had the same effect on her that she had on me.

I got careless.

I tried holding her hand in school.

"Slow down, Miss Lucy," she said. "Slow down."

I said I wanted to see her house.

Her room.

Her bed.

She told me they weren't worth seeing.

I asked her if there'd been other girls before me.

She laughed and said yes.

I asked: "Am I the second? The seventh? The thirtieth?"

But she didn't tell me any more than that.

I had told her about Lily White, and now whenever I didn't want to do something she wanted me to do, she'd tease me about getting back together with Lily White, about how we'd be perfect together.

"Lucy likes to lick Lily," she'd tease.

"Don't be mean to me," I'd say.

"I'm not," she said. "It's a joke."

Later, we'd be with each other and it would seem right—the perfect rhythm, the desire clouding us. Afterward, she'd hold me close—the perfect daze—and she'd say, "Miss Lucy, you and I are a pair, aren't we?"

But then she'd tell me not to be so attached.

The more this happened, the deeper I fell in love with her.

The more she made me want it, the more I wanted it.

"Open your eyes," Teddy told me, one of the few times I talked to him.

But that wasn't the problem.

My eyes were wide open.

Seeing her.

All the conversations in our relationship started to be about our relationship.

I was always the one who brought it up.

"What am I to you?" I would ask.

"Oh Lord," she'd groan. "Not again."

"Are we girlfriends? *Lovers?* Nothing at all? What?"

"I'm Ashley and you're Miss Lucy. Isn't that enough?"

"No, it's not enough!" I'd protest, not even sure what I was defending.

"I don't need this, Miss Lucy. Really."

> Miss Lucy had a steamboat
> The steamboat had a bell
> Miss Lucy went to heaven
> and the steamboat went to

"What are you mumbling?"

"Nothing."

"C'mon."

"I love you."

"No."

"I do."

> *Hello, operator*
> *Please give me number nine*
> *And if you disconnect me*
> *I'll chop off your*

The kissing was supposed to be the escape. The kissing was supposed to be the moment when nothing in the world mattered but us. The kissing was supposed to take me away from all the problems. All the thoughts. All the doubts.

But now when I kissed her, I was always measuring how much of her was there. And I was wondering how much of me was left.

> *Behind the 'frigerator*
> *There was a piece of glass*
> *Miss Lucy sat upon it*
> *And it went right up her*

It was, I thought, a simple equation:

You find the right person.

You do the right things.

And from that, everything goes right.

Like you have a contract with the universe, and these are the terms.

I had no doubt Ashley was the right person.

I had to hope I was doing the right things.
But everything wasn't going right.
Some things were.
But not everything.

> *Ask me no more questions*
> *And I'll tell you no more lies*
> *The boys are in the bathroom*
> *Zipping up their*

Miss Lucy disappears from her own story.

> *Flies are in the belfry*
> *Bees are in the park*
> *And boys and girls are kissing*
> *In the D-A-R-K*

I felt I was disappearing from my own story.

> *D-A-R-K*

I had no control over my own story.

> *D-A-R-K*

It was hers.

> *DARK DARK DARK*

I had to take my SATs a third time.
Ashley knew this. I'd told her.

Before I went in, I texted her: WHAT DO YOU WANT TO DO TONIGHT? It was a Saturday, and I thought we'd made plans. After a few months of going out, this was pretty routine.

Of course, I forgot to turn off my phone. So ten minutes into the SATs, my bag starts to chirp, and it will not shut up. Now, I knew I wasn't supposed to take out my phone during the SATs, and I swear to this day that my intention was just to silence it until I was done penciling in those stupid bubbles. But as I went to hit the off button, I happened to look at the message on the screen:

WE HAVE TO TALK.

The test proctor was immediately yelling at me, asking what the hell did I think I was doing, as if I'd been about to call some math expert for help. I threw the phone back in my bag, but I couldn't get rid of the message as easily. It was like every problem on the SATs became my problem.

5. WHAT DO YOU WANT TO DO TONIGHT?: WE HAVE TO TALK : : ASHLEY, I CARE ABOUT YOU:

    a) LUCY, I CARE ABOUT YOU, TOO
    b) LUCY, WE'RE SO COMPLETELY OVER, IT'S NOT FUNNY
    c) LUCY, YOU'RE THE LOVE OF MY LIFE
    d) STEAMBOAT, I CARE ABOUT YOU, TOO

6. Which of the following phrases does not belong with the others?

    a) WE HAVE TO SEE MORE OF EACH OTHER
    b) WE HAVE TO TALK

```
      c) WE HAVE TO REMEMBER TO PICK UP A MOVIE
      d) WE HAVE TO BE TOGETHER ALWAYS


    12. If the diameter of a cone is doubled, its
volume:

      a) will quadruple
      b) will not be enough to save your
         relationship with Ashley
      c) will halve
      d) will stay the same
```

Of course, all the right answers were (b).

I might as well have used that number-two pencil to fill in the hollow dots that my eyes, my ears, my mouth, and my heart had become. Not only had I not seen it coming, but I had seen its opposite coming instead.

Doofus, I said to myself. *Idiot*.

I started crying in the middle of my third try at the SATs and I couldn't stop. I had to leave, and there was no way to explain to the proctor how a single sentence had stumped me more than any test question ever would.

All I really needed was the confirmation. And all I needed for the confirmation was a simple two-letter word spoken in her voice. I called her as soon as I got to the parking lot. I knew she'd see my number on her phone, so when she answered, she'd be answering me. So the way she said that first word—*hi*—made the landslide complete. Her *hi* wasn't high at all—no, this *hi* was *lowwwwwwww*. The kind of *hi* that says *I've already scattered the ashes of our relationship somewhere over the land of yesterday*. All in two letters.

I began to cry again, and she told me she'd known I was going to be this way. I cried some more. She mentioned something about me still being her best friend in town. Not her best friend, mind you—her best friend *in town*. I wiped some snot with my sleeve. She asked me wasn't I supposed to be in the SATs right now? I just lost it and took that phone and threw it right at my car. Which is how I managed to lose a girlfriend, break a phone, and crack a windshield all at the same time.

And then I drove over to her house.

I didn't make it past the front door.

"What are you doing here?" she asked, stepping onto the porch and pulling the door shut behind her. "And what the hell happened to your car?"

"What do you think I'm doing here?" I said, the tears already coming.

"It doesn't have to be like this," she said, completely bored with the whole thing.

"Really? What can it be like? Tell me. I'd really like to know."

"You see, this is why it was never going to work."

"Because I'm upset that you're dumping me? That's why it was never going to work?"

"You were always too into it."

"But you said we were a pair! You were into it, too."

"Yeah, but not like you. And I wasn't always telling the truth."

It had never occurred to me that a person could know all the right things to say and deploy them to get what she wanted, without having to mean any of it.

Dear Lord, I staggered then. Staggered back. Staggered away from her. Staggered to my car and cried for a good five minutes before I could get my key in the ignition. When I got home, I staggered past my mother, who called out, asking what was wrong. My breathing was staggered. My memory was staggered. And there was no way to get it right again.

I was waiting for her to call and say she'd made a mistake.

That was my own mistake.

I didn't want to go to school, but when my mother threatened to stay home with me if I didn't go, I knew I didn't have a choice.

"Is it some boy?" she asked, unable to keep the hope out of her voice.

"No, I'm just garden-variety suicidal," I told her.

"Fine," she replied, annoyed. "Be that way."

I tried to shut myself down completely, put up my best screen-saver personality to coast through the day. I didn't want to see her. I was desperate to see her. I wanted to hold it together. I wanted to melt down right at her feet and scream, *Look what you've done to me*.

I was going to skip lunch entirely, but Teddy found me and steered me toward his table.

"Spill," he said.

"I can't," I told him.

"Why not?"

"Because if I start, I might not stop."

That's what it felt like—that if I let a little of the hurt out, it would keep pouring out until I was a deflated balloon of a person, with a big monster of hurt in front of me.

"You know what?" I said. "I'm not Miss Lucy at all. I'm the goddamn steamboat."

"Come again?" Teddy said with his usual shoulder-tilt pout.

"Let's just say this is *not* heaven," I said with a sigh.

Heron, of course, knew exactly what I was talking about.

"It's just that Mercury's in retrograde," she said.

"This has nothing to do with a fucking planet," I groaned.

"Down, girl," Teddy sassed. "Down."

I put my head in my hands and took a deep breath, hearing the air suck against my palms.

I felt Teddy pat my back, then start to rub it. Mmmmmm.

"A little better now?" he asked.

I nodded a little and he moved to my neck.

"Let it go," he said. "Let it go."

I tried to. I wanted to block it out.

Miss Lucy had a steamboat. Miss Lucy had a steamboat.

"What are you saying?" Teddy whispered in my ear.

I lifted my head and told him. Then Heron and I explained what it meant.

"So you've sat on the glass," Teddy said.

"Repeatedly."

"And, let me get this straight, the boys are in the bathroom—"

"The boys don't really matter right now."

"There will be other girls," Heron comforted.

"I don't want other girls!" I cried.

What I meant then: *I only want Ashley.*

I couldn't stop thinking about her. My body missed her. My mind reeled at her absence. I was a fucking wreck. It wasn't pretty, and as much as I wanted to believe she was doing it to me, I had to begin to admit that I was doing it to myself, too.

Why is self-preservation so much more of a bitch when it's your mental health that's involved? I mean, if there really *was* a piece of glass on my chair, I'd damn well make sure that I didn't sit on it twice. If a steamboat *was* sinking, I'd know enough to head to the lifeboat. But a broken heart? At first I gave in to the temptation to think, nah, there was nothing I could do about it. I'd have to keep sitting on glass until someone was nice enough to take the glass away from my seat.

Then I thought, *To hell with that.* I actually had to think of it in terms of sitting on glass for it to work.

"What's up with the whole couple thing anyway?" I asked Teddy and Heron at lunch a week or so after Ashley had dumped me.

"What do you mean?" Teddy asked back.

"I mean, why is everyone so brainwashed into believing that they have to be in a relationship with one other person? Look at us, Teddy. If anyone were to tell us that the whole girl-boy thing was natural and anything else was unnatural, we'd know they were completely wrong. But have them tell us that every person needs to be with another person in order to be happy, and we nod along like it's the most obvious thing in the world. But there's no *reason* for it, is there? It's not a proven *truth.* It's just some thing that our culture has come to spin itself around, mostly so we'll procreate, and we're the dupes who fall for it over and over and over again."

"I thought you were over the breakup," Teddy said hesitantly.

"*I am,*" I insisted. "Can't you see that this is more than that?"

Teddy clearly couldn't see, because he was looking at me like I was fifty-eight varieties of crazy all at once.

Heron, however, surprised me.

"You're totally right," she said. "And I'm tired of it, too."

When I realized I was into girls, it was scary to let go of all the things I was supposed to be and all the things I was supposed to want. It's like you're a character in this book that everyone around you is writing, and suddenly you have to say, *I'm sorry, but this role isn't right for me.* And you have to start writing your own life and doing your own thing. That was hard enough. But that was nothing—nothing, I tell you—compared to the idea that I could let go of the desire to have a girlfriend. Maybe not forever. Maybe forever. Certainly for now. Talk about something that had been *ingrained*. I wasn't letting go of love or sex or the idea of companionship. I was just rejecting the package in which it was being sold to me. I was going to say it was okay to be alone, when it felt like everyone in the world was saying that it wasn't okay to be alone, that I had to always want someone else, that the desire had to fuel me.

I didn't want to feel like I needed it anymore. Because I didn't. Really, I didn't.

Ashley started fooling around with Lily White. She didn't tell me this, but I could figure it out easily enough. Lily White was more scared of me than ever. And she'd started to smell a little like Ashley's shampoo.

Betrayal. Lust. Secrecy. Devotion. I think we do these things to feel more alive. When the truth is that alive is alive—you can feel it in anything, if you give it a chance.

I thought more about Miss Lucy.

I'd never pictured her with anybody else, just her steamboat and her bell. Trying to keep things together, even when the world was constantly throwing glass under her ass.

"Do you think there was a real Miss Lucy?" I asked Heron.

"I don't know," she said.

"I want to find out," I told her.

The trouble I felt coming when I first met Ashley was nothing compared to the trouble I felt when I first realized I didn't need her or anyone like her. People fall hard for the notion of falling, and saying you want no part of it will only get you sent to the loony bin. C'mon, you've seen the movie: As soon as the headstrong girl announces she's not going to fall in love, you know she'll be falling in love before the final credits. That's the way the story goes. Only it's not going to be my story. I am taking my story in my own hands. I don't care for the way it's supposed to go. Some people find happily ever after in being part of a couple, and for them, I say, *good for you*. But that's no reason we should all have to do it. That's no reason that every goddamn song and story has to say we should.

I tried to explain myself to people.

"You don't know what you're missing," Teddy, who usually had about four crushes going on at the same time, told me. "It's the best excuse in the world for getting absolutely nothing done."

When I called my sister at college and told her about my revelation, she acted like I'd announced I was shipping myself off to a nunnery. (Which would only be another form of crushing, if you ask me.)

"Did someone hurt you that badly?" she asked.

And I told her, no, it wasn't that.

"You *want* to be single?"

I said yes. And then I told her that I thought *single* was a stupid term. It made it sound like you were unattached to anyone, unconnected to anything. I preferred the term *singular*. As in *individual*.

"Does this have anything to do with . . ."

My sister couldn't bring herself to say it, but I was still impressed. Besides a few gender-neutral terms (like *someone*, see above), she'd never really acknowledged that I was a [whatever term you want for lesbian].

"No, it doesn't," I told her. "I'd feel this way even if I were into guys."

"Well," she said, "just don't tell Mom. You'll never hear the end of it."

I didn't tell Mom. I did, however, finally speak to Ashley again. I couldn't avoid her forever. As soon as Ashley sensed me not wanting her anymore, she stepped right back into my line of vision.

"I miss you," she said.

"That's special," I told her.

She laughed, and this time the laugh meant nothing to me.

"There's something I have to tell you," she said.

"Don't," I said.

"You know about me and Lily?"

"Yeah, I know."

"I'm sorry. It just happened."

"Let it, then. Why not let it?"

It felt so good not to care. Not to need.

"Miss Lucy," she said. Quietly. Sweetly. Trying to pull me back in.

"Miss Lucy's gone to heaven," I told her.

You never think of heaven in terms of who likes who, or who's with who, or whether this crush works, or whether the sex is good. In heaven you don't worry about what you're going to wear, or what you have to say, or whether someone loves you back, or whether someone will be with you when you die. In heaven, you just live. Because it's heaven.

"Let's go on a trip," I told Teddy and Heron. "Let's drive until we find Miss Lucy."

The three of us. The four of us. The hundred of us. The thousands of us.

You see, *us* doesn't need a particular number to make it fit.

I'm tired of convincing myself otherwise. I can put that energy to better use.

Let the boys and girls go on kissing in the dark.

I want more.

THE ALUMNI INTERVIEW

It is never easy to have a college interview with your closeted boyfriend's father. Would I have applied to this university if I had known that of all the alumni in the greater metropolitan area, it would choose Mr. Wright to find me worthy or unworthy? Maybe. But maybe not.

Thom took it worse than I did. We had been making out in the boys' room, with him standing on the toilet so no one would know we were in the stall together. Even though I was younger, he was a little shorter and had much better balance than I did. Dating him, I'd learned to kiss quietly, and from different inclinations.

He found the letter as he searched through my bag for some gum.

"You heard from them?" he asked.

I nodded.

"An interview?"

"Yeah," I answered casually. "With your dad."

"Yeah, right."

The bell had rung. The bathroom sounded empty. I looked under the stall door to see if anyone's feet were around, then opened it.

"No, really," I said.

His face turned urinal-white.

"You can't."

"I have to. I can't exactly refuse an alumni interview."

He thought about it for a second.

"Shit."

I had almost met Mr. Wright before. He had come home early one day when his office's air-conditioning system had broken down. Luckily, Thom's room is right over the garage, so the garage door heralded his arrival with an appropriately earthquakian noise. Thom was pulling on my shirt at the time, and as a result, I lost two buttons. At first, I figured it was just his mom. But the footsteps beat out a different tune. I did the mature, responsible thing, which was to hide under the bed for the next three hours. Happily, Thom hid with me. We found ways to occupy ourselves. Then, once Thom had moved downstairs and the family was safely wrapped up in dinner, I climbed out the window. I could've gone out the window earlier, but I'd been having a pretty good time.

The trick was getting Thom to enjoy it, too. I wasn't his first boyfriend, but I was the first he could admit to himself. We'd reached the stage where he felt comfortable liberating his affections when we were alone together, or even within our closest circle of friends. But outside that circle, he got nervous. He became paralyzed at the very thought of his parents discovering his—*our*—secret.

We'd been going out without going out for three months.

I'd picked my first choice for college before Thom and I had gotten together, long before I'd known his father had gone to the same school. Thom couldn't believe I wanted to go to a place that had helped spawn the person his father had become.

"Your dad wasn't in the drama program," I pointed out. "And I think he was there before Vietnam."

It helped that my first-choice college was in the same city as Thom's. We'd vowed that we wouldn't think or talk about such things. But of course we did. All the time.

We were trapped in the limbo between where we were and where we wanted to be. The limbo of our age.

The day of the alumni interview, we were both as jittery as a tightrope walker with vertigo. We spun through the day at school, the clock hands spiraling us to certain doom. We found every possible excuse to touch each other—hand on shoulder, fingers on back, stolen kisses, loving looks. Everything that would stop the moment his father walked into the room.

He gave me a ride home, then drove back to his house. I counted to a hundred, then walked over.

Thom answered the door. We'd agreed on this beforehand. I didn't want to be in his house without seeing him. I wanted to know he was there.

"I've got it!" he yelled to the study as he opened the door.

"Here we go," I said.

He leaned into me and whispered, "I love you."

And I whispered, "I love you, too."

We didn't have time for any more than that. So we said all that needed to be said.

I'd never been in Mr. Wright's study before. The man fit in well with the furniture. Sturdy. Wooden. Upright.

It is a strange thing to meet your boyfriend's father when the father doesn't know you're his son's boyfriend—or even that his son *has* a boyfriend. It puts you at an advantage—you know more than he does—and it also puts you at a disadvantage. The things you know are things you can't under any circumstances let him know.

I was not ordinarily known for my discretion. But I was trying to make an exception in this case. It seemed exceptional.

Thom stood in the doorway, hovering.

"Dad, this is Ian."

"Have a seat, Ian," the man said, no handshake. "Thank you, Thom."

Thom stayed one beat too long, that last beat of linger that we'd grown accustomed to, the sign of an unwanted good-bye. But then the situation hit him again, and he left the room without a farewell glance.

I turned to Mr. Wright as the door closed behind him.

I can do this, I thought. Then: *And even if I can't, I have to.*

Mr. Wright had clearly done the alumni interview thing a hundred times before. As if reciting a speech beamed in from central campus, he talked about how this interview was not supposed to be a formal one; it was all about getting to know me, and me getting to know the college where he had spent some of the best years of his life. He had a few questions to ask, and he was sure that I had many questions to ask as well.

In truth, I had already visited the campus twice and knew people who went there. I didn't have a single question to ask. Or, more accurately, the questions I wanted to ask didn't have anything to do with the university in question.

Thom says you've never in all his life hugged him. Why is that?

What can I do to make you see how wonderful he is? If I told you the way I still smile after he kisses me, is there any possible way you'd understand what he means to me?

Don't you know how wrong it is when you wave a twenty-dollar bill in front of your son and tell him that when he gets a girlfriend, you'll be happy to pay for the first date?

And then I'd add:

My father isn't like you at all. So don't tell me it's normal.

I am not by nature an angry person. But as this man kept saying he wanted to get to know me, I wanted to throw the phrase right back at him. How could he possibly get to know me when he didn't want to know his son?

Taking out a legal pad and consulting a folder with my transcript in it, he asked me about school and classes. And as I prattled on about AP Biology and my English awards, I kept thinking about the word *transcript*. What exactly did it transcribe? It was a bloodless, calendar version of my life. It transcribed nothing but the things I was doing in order to get into a good college. It was the biography of my paper self. Getting to know it wasn't getting to know me at all.

Sitting in that room, talking to Mr. Wright, I knew I had to get all of my identities in order. I realized how many identities I had, at a time when I really should have been focusing on having one.

"I see that you haven't taken economics," Mr. Wright said.

"No," I replied.

"Why not?" he harrumphed.

I explained that our school only offered one economics class, and I had a conflict. A complete lie, but how would he know?

"I see."

He wrote something down, then told me how important

economics was to an education, and how he would have never gotten through college—not to mention life—without a firm foundation in economics.

I nodded. I agreed. I succumbed to the lecture, because really I didn't have any choice. Judgmental. I considered the word *judgmental*. The mental state of always judging. His tone. I knew he wasn't singling me out. I knew this was probably the way he always was.

There were times I had gotten mad at Thom. Argument mad. Cutting-comment mad. Because his inability to be open made me a little closed. I didn't want to be a conditional boyfriend. I didn't want to be anybody's secret. As much as I said I understood, I never entirely understood.

Can't you just tell them? I'd ask. After they became the excuse for why we couldn't go out on Saturday. After they became the reason he pulled his hand away from mine as we were walking through town—*what if they drove by?* But then I'd feel bad, feel wrong. Because I knew this was not the way he wanted it to be. That even though we were sixteen, we were still that one leap away from independence. We were still caught on the dependence side, staring over the divide.

It was different now, bearing the brunt of his father's disapproval.

I understood. Not all of it. But a little more.

". . . too many of you students ignore economics. You dilly-dally. You spend your time on such expendable things. Like Thom. You know Thom, right? No focus. He has no focus. He wouldn't be right for this university. You show more promise, but I have to say, you need to make sure you don't spend time on expendable things. . . ."

And suddenly I was sick of it.

I looked to the door and saw something. A shadow in the key-hole. And I knew. Thom had never left me. He was on the outside of the door, holding his breath for me. Trying to keep quiet. Staying quiet, because his father was around.

I was sick of it.

The economics lecture was over. Mr. Wright didn't alter his tone when he asked, "What are your interests?"

"Your son in my room," I said.

"Excuse me?"

"The sun and the moon," I said. "Astronomy."

Mr. Wright looked pleased. "I didn't know kids liked astron-omy anymore. When I was a child, we all had telescopes. Now you just have telephones and televisions instead."

"You couldn't be more right, sir." I nodded emphatically, as if I believed for a second that he hadn't watched television or spoken on the telephone as a child. "A telescope is a fine instrument. And there's something about the stars. . . ." I paused dramatically.

"Yes?"

"Well, there's something about the stars that makes you realize both the smallness and the enormity of everything, isn't there?"

Thom had first told me this as we lay on our backs on a golf course outside of town, too late for the twilight, but early enough to catch the rise of the moon, the pinprick arrival of the stars. His words were like a grasping.

Now here was his father, agreeing with him, through me.

"Yes, yes, absolutely," Mr. Wright said.

I looked to the keyhole, to Thom's shadow there. Knowing he was near. Speaking to him in this code.

Saying to his father what I've said to him.

"Sometimes I wish we could open ourselves up to each other as much as we do to the sky. To the smallness and the enormity."

This time, I lost Mr. Wright. He looked at me as if I'd just spoken in an absurd tongue.

"I see," he said, looking back at his notes. "And do you have any other interests?"

Must interests be interesting? That is, must they be interesting to someone other than yourself? This is why I hate these interviews, these applications. *List your interests.* I wanted to say, *Look, interests aren't things that can be listed. My interests are impulses, are moods, are neverending. Sometimes it's as simple as Thom holding my hand. Sometimes it's as complicated as wanting to be able to hold his hand in front of his father. That want is an interest of mine.*

"I swim," I said.

"Are you on the swim team?"

"No."

"Why is that?"

"I like to do it alone."

"I see."

He wrote something else down. *Not a team player,* no doubt.

"Thom is on the swim team," he added.

"I know," I said.

"Very competitive." As if that was the marker of a fine activity.

"So I've heard." I had grown so tired of competitions. Of sacrificing the nights of stargazing in order to make the paper self as impressive as possible.

"Do you know Thom well?" Mr. Wright asked.

"We're friends," I said. Not a lie, but not the whole truth.

"Well, do me a favor and make sure he stays on track."

"Oh, I will."

It had now gone from uncomfortable to downright fierce. He picked up my transcript again, frowned, and asked, "What is the GSA?"

I tried to imagine him coming to one of our Gay-Straight Alliance meetings. I tried to imagine that he would understand if I told him what it was. I tried to think of a way to avoid his shiver of revulsion, his dismissive disdain.

Thom had tried to signal him once. Had left the pink triangle pin that I'd placed on his bag after a meeting, and he hadn't taken it off when he got home. But it hadn't worked. Mr. Wright had brushed right past it. He hadn't noticed or hadn't said. When all Thom wanted was for him to notice without being told.

"GSA stands for God Smiles Always, sir," I said with my most sincere expression.

"I didn't know the high school had one of those."

"It's pretty new, sir."

"How did it start?"

"Because of the school musical," I earnestly explained. "A lot of the kids in the musical wanted to start it."

"Really?"

"It was *Jesus Christ Superstar*, sir. I think we were all moved by how much of a superstar Jesus was. It made us want to work to make God smile."

"And the school is okay with this?" Mr. Wright asked, his eyebrow raising slightly, a vague irritation in his voice.

"Yes, sir. It's all about bringing people together."

"It says here you were on the dance committee for the GSA?"

I nodded, imagining Thom's reaction behind the door. "I was one of the coordinators," I elaborated. "We wanted to create a wholesome atmosphere for our fellow students. We only played

Christian dance music. It's like Christian rock music, only the beat is a little faster. The lyrics are mostly the same."

"Did Thom go to that dance?"

"Yes, sir. I believe I saw him there." *In fact, he was my date. Afterward, we had sex.*

"It also says you were involved in something called the Pride March?"

"Yes. We dress up as a pride of lions and we march. It's a school spirit thing. Our mascot is a lion."

"I thought it was an eagle?"

"It used to be an eagle. But then our principal's kid saw *The Lion King* and got hooked. You know how these things work."

He did not look amused. "Do you march in costume?"

"Yes. But we don't wear the heads."

"Why not?"

"Because we're proud. We want people to know who we are."

"It says the Pride March is tied to Coming Out Day."

Damn. The transcript might as well have been written in lavender ink.

I faked a laugh. "Oh, that. It's another school spirit thing. First day of the football season, someone dresses up as a lion and comes out from under the bleachers onto the field. If we see its shadow, we know the season will be a long one. If not, we know it's pretty much over before it's begun. The whole school gets really into it."

"I can't recall Thom mentioning that."

"He hasn't? Maybe he thought it was a secret."

"I know what's going on here."

Mr. Wright put down the transcript.

Now it was my turn to say, "Excuse me?"

"I know what's going on here," Mr. Wright said again, more pronounced. "And I don't like it one bit."

"I'm sorry, sir, but . . ."

He stood up from his chair. "I will *not* be ridiculed in my own house. That you should have the *presumption* to apply to my alma mater and then to sit there and *mock* me. I know what you are, and I will not stand for it here."

I wish I could say that I hurled a response right back at him. But mostly, I was stunned. To have such a blast directed at me. To be yelled at.

I couldn't move. I couldn't figure out what to do.

Then the door opened, and Thom said, "Stop it. Stop it right now."

Now Mr. Wright and I had something in common—disbelief. But even though I had disbelief, I also had faith. In Thom.

"If you say one more word, I'm going to scream," he said to his father. "I don't give a shit what you say to me, but you leave Ian out of it, okay? You're being a total asshole, and that's not okay."

Mr. Wright started to yell. But it was empty yelling. Desperate yelling, mostly focusing on Thom's *foul language*. While he yelled, Thom came over to me and took my hand. I stood up and together we faced his father. And his father fell silent. And his father began to cry.

As if the world had ended.

And it had, in a way.

I could feel Thom shaking, the tremors of that world exploding. As we stood there. As we watched. As we broke free from limbo.

And I wanted to say, *All you really need to get to know me is to know that I love your son. And if you get to know your son, you will know what that means.*

But the words were no longer mine to say.

Except here. I am writing this to let you know why it is likely that you received a very harsh alumni interview report about me. I'm hoping my campus interview will provide a contrast. (Thom and I will be heading up there next week.) I do not hold it against your university that a person like Mr. Wright should have received such a poor education. I understand those were different times then, and I am glad these are different times now.

It is never easy to have a college interview with your closeted boyfriend's father. It is never easy, I'm sure, to conduct a college interview with your closeted son's boyfriend. And, I am positive, it is least easy of all to be the boy in the hallway, listening in.

But if I've learned one thing, it's this:

It's not the easy things that let you get to know a person.

Know, and love.

THE GOOD WITCH

It was a mistake from the start. I see that now, and the really twisted thing is that I saw it then. But once you utter the words "Will you go to the prom with me?" there's no way back. The wheels have left the ground and you're officially over the cliff.

I asked Sally Huston to go to the prom because I was bored in bio class. There's no other way to explain it. I was bored . . . she was sitting next to me . . . I got to thinking . . . and that was that. I wasn't dating anyone—I'd already gone out with this girl Nina for like two years, and once that was over I thought I could coast until college. I didn't realize I was gay yet, so it wasn't like I was taking a boy to the prom. I had all these friends-who-were-girls, but I knew that if I asked one of them to the prom, the other six would be bitter. So that left me looking for someone fringe, someone safe, someone who wouldn't make a big deal about it. Sally and I passed notes all the time, mostly because the alternative was paying attention in class. I knew she wasn't dating anyone, since she'd broken up with this guy Mark at about the same time I'd broken up with Nina. So I just put it in a note—*Hey, wanna go to prom?* I don't even think I bothered to fold it. But the way she reacted, you would've thought I'd sent it over on a velvet pillow. Her eyes lit up the moment she saw the sentence. I mean, I wasn't actually watching as she read the note. But the next time I looked over, her eyes were still lit. She wrote back—*Are you sure?* And this time I didn't even bother writing it down. I just said, "Of course I am," real low so the teacher wouldn't hear. I was relieved to have the whole thing over with.

By the time lunch hit, everyone knew. I could tell because now I had seven friends-who-were-girls pissed at me, each in her own special way.

"It's no big deal," I said.

"You better shut up, because you're only going to make it worse," my friend Theresa warned me.

"But I thought you guys liked Sally," I said.

"That is *so* not the point," Theresa replied—I think she actually sighed when she said it.

There were only about three weeks to go before prom, which meant the seven of them had to grab any available guy to be their dates. Most of them ended up with juniors—and not the kind of juniors who act like they're already seniors, more the kind that you can never remember whether they're a sophomore or a junior or even a freshman. It was clear that the girls would be the ones to buy the corsages and the boutonnieres. And they were not going to ask me to come along when they did.

Sally was cool about the whole thing, at least at first. Most of our conversations about it happened in written form, while the respiratory system was being explained. The limo logistics, the cummerbund/gown coordination—we figured everything out. If asked, we said we were going as friends.

The girls in my group circled their limos and made their plans without me. I didn't have any real guy friends to speak of—or, at least, to speak *to*—so Sally and I ended up getting a limo by ourselves. The price of everything blew my mind, but Sally was good about splitting it. She said she knew it was stupid to get a limo when both of us had cars, but she thought it wouldn't be prom without one.

The day of the prom, the limo picked me up first. I was wearing my dad's tux, feeling massively uncomfortable but ready to hang out and have a good time. I rode over to her house with her corsage next to me in its plastic deli container, the big-ass ninja pins stuck through the stems. As I was walking up Sally's front steps, I felt like something out of a syndicated sitcom, stuck in a lost episode of *The Brady Bunch*. Sure enough, her dad opened the door and gave me a dad handshake. Her mom fluttered around like she was the one going to the prom. Sally was nowhere in sight. I waited in the front hall, mustering charm for the gushing parents. Then I heard the creak of floorboards. I looked up, and Sally's dress appeared at the top of the stairs, with her body somewhere in it.

She looked like Glinda the Good Witch. There's no other way to describe it. The description hit immediately—I mean, I explicitly thought, *Holy shit, she looks like Glinda the Good Witch.* And there was no letting go of it. I have never in my life seen so much pink. It was poofing everywhere. She had to turn slightly to the side to get down the stairs.

This was a girl I'd only seen in jeans before. A girl who used words like *fuckbucket* in her notes to me. A girl who I *knew* listened to Led Zeppelin.

She was wearing pink lipstick. She was wearing so much blush that it made *me* blush. And her hair was frozen in this hairdon't that would have made Little Miss Sunshine turn dark. Her mother started snapping photos and her dad looked all misty and I hid every ounce of my laughter behind the broadest smile I could possibly manage.

"You look beautiful," I said, when what I really meant was, *This is one image I'll never, ever forget.*

She told me I looked handsome, and then teetered there (her shoes were pink, too, and left her stilted). Her mom shot a look at my hands and I offered up the corsage. The plastic took about two minutes to open, and then I didn't know what to do. All the places that I would've put the corsage were covered with sequins, and since I'd never really experienced sequin-pin interaction before, I wasn't sure where to attach the damn flowers. To be honest, the pins scared the hell out of me, because they seemed like something from a butterfly collector's table, and the last thing I wanted to do in front of Sally's parents was draw blood.

Mr. Huston, God bless him, came to my rescue, saying, "Honey, why don't you pin it on? It looks kind of dangerous."

I stood there staring, because now I was seeing—no—could it really be?—*eyeshadow.*

We took about two hundred pictures—I think we were posed in each room of the house, as well as the backyard and front yard. I figured we might miss the prom entirely, and I can't say that I entirely minded. Sally had gotten me a boutonniere that was nearly the size of the corsage. It was made of magenta roses. Magenta.

When her parents were finally secured back inside the house, I half expected and fully hoped that Sally would say, "I can't believe my mom made me wear this dress! Hold on a second while I get my real clothes from behind this potted geranium."

Instead she said, "We're going to have the most wonderful night. And I'm so happy I'm sharing it with you." I looked to see if she was using a Hallmark card as a crib sheet.

The limo driver got out of his car as we approached. When Sally got to the door, he had her lift the front of the dress, bend one knee, lift one leg, lift another part of the dress, turn, squeeze, lift the other leg, lean, and squeeze some more in order to fit it all in. I watched as Sally billowed and twisted, then—once the door was closed without incident—I walked to the other side and squeezed myself in.

On the way over, we talked about other people's dates and other people's plans. Safe ground. Then Sally said, "Isn't this a great dress?"

And I said, "It sure is something."

Then, from somewhere underneath her linebacker shoulder pads and soufflé sleeves, her hand reached over and grasped mine.

And I thought, *Oh-kay* . . .

Her thumb slowly stroked my thumb.

And I thought, *Oh no*.

"You're so cute," she said.

"You, too," I offered. Then I added, "We're almost there—I'd better fix my hair," and moved my hand away to do it.

I was hoping that Sally's Glindawear happened to be the fashion for our year, that some other girls would dress in a similar way so Sally wouldn't stand out so much. When we got to the prom, though, I saw this wasn't meant to be. Yes, there were certainly other girls in pink. And, yes, there were some girls whose dresses looked like they were made of icing. But Sally was the Marie Antoinette of this particular court. And I could've been fine with that—I swear I could've been fine with that—but when the time came for us to take another round of pictures, Sally not only bought the set of sixty-four, but she also ran her finger over my chin after she straightened my tie, giving me this look that I can only call *amateur seductive*.

I knew I was in trouble.

Luckily for me, tables were five couples each, so Theresa, Liz, and their respective dates had to break off from the rest of their posse to sit with me and Sally. The look on Theresa's face when she saw Sally was probably the second-most memorable image of the night—I could read Theresa better than I could read myself, and at that moment, she had shock, terror, high hilarity, and a sense of cosmic justice all written across her face. But she didn't miss a beat. She headed over to us, hugged Sally's crinoline shoulders, and then, when Sally was turned away, gave me a look that was pure *Oh. My. God.*

Theresa's date was a junior with the unbelievable name of Leighton Noble, a cartoonist for the school newspaper who, in one year's time, would discover both The Smiths and recreational drugs, letting his hair grow long in the front and his moods grow long in the back, becoming the kind of boy I now wish I had dated in high school. Liz's date was a junior named Phil—I can't remember his last name, but he was something like third alternate on the debate team. He spent pretty much the whole night staring at his place card, as if he'd never before realized how fascinating the spelling of his name could be. There were two other couples at the table, but they were couples with each other and not with us, so they stuck to their end and we stuck to ours.

Sally tucked so much of her dress underneath her in order to fit on the chair that it must have felt like sitting on a phone book. We were served a salad entirely defined by lettuce and a piece of chicken that was cold at the core. There was a band, not a DJ, and at first it seemed like they had mistaken our prom for a thirty-fifth anniversary party; as we ate, the air was awash with songs from our mothers' daytime soap operas. When the middle strains of "Tonight I Celebrate My Love with You" crescendoed, Sally actually leaned over onto my shoulder. Theresa nearly laughed her lettuce out through her nose.

There is no way to say "I'd like to point out that we're not on a date" without sounding like a complete asshole. And I hadn't yet discovered that sometimes you need to sound like a complete asshole early on in order to prevent sounding like an even more complete asshole further down the road. So I just patted her taffeta and let her lean.

Once the dinner had been cleared and the prom committee had congratulated itself, the music picked up and we picked ourselves up to go with it. At Theresa and Liz's urging, Sally kicked off her heels, which meant that the frosted peak of her hair was now level with my nose. As if to atone for the waiting-room music of the past, the band went into a (by my count) thirteen-song Motown medley—it had nothing to do with our high school years, but at least we could dance to it. Sally did not leave my side, but neither did Theresa (whose date only knew the box-step) or Liz (whose date was still at the table). The first song in the medley was "Ain't Too Proud to Beg," and I made sure that when I got down on my knees, it was Theresa I was facing. She got the message, and I knew she forgave me for not asking her. She wouldn't abandon me. So the four of us heard it through the grapevine together. We stopped in the name of love together. We even (good lord) just called to say I love you together. It wasn't until we were about to be signed, sealed, delivered that Sally tried to wedge herself between me and the other girls, tripping over her dress to grab hold of my waist. It wasn't a slow song, but clearly her patience in waiting for a slow song was starting to wear thin. We were both sweating now from the dancing, and I could see in her eyes a determination that bio class had never, ever elicited.

"Sally . . . ," I said over the music.

"Damon . . . ," she said back, pulling a little closer.

Then (hey, the good lord *is* good) "Twist and Shout" started, and there was no way to pretend it was an intimacy-inducing tune. I tried to twist in time with her, but we were always just a little off. When the medley was finally over, I gasped for some water and headed back to the table.

I thought that maybe if we could talk normally, it would all go back to normal. But it soon became apparent that I was speaking to some prom version of Sally, without being able to summon a prom version of myself. I tried talking about college next year, about how weird it was to be facing the last of our final exams, about how I couldn't believe that Nina wouldn't even come over to say hi. I thought Sally would bring up her own ex, so we could bond over our jiltedness in a friend kind of way. But she just said she had never understood why Nina and I were together in the first place, and that I deserved *much better than that*. Then she said, "Let's not talk about Nina," and asked me if I was ready to dance again. A slow song had just come on.

Clearly, Sally thought this dance was going to seal the deal. She wrapped her arms around my neck and dangled there, my very own new-girlfriend necklace. Usually when I slow-danced with Theresa or Liz or one of the other girls, we'd joke with each other, hanging out. But Sally had no desire for banter. She was staring at me so intently. She didn't even look happy. Instead, she looked determined to be happy. I was the only thing standing in the way.

My arms were around her back, caught in the bubblegum folds. I knew if I'd wanted her, if I'd really wanted her, my hands would've moved up—they would have wanted to touch skin. I know that thrill now—of sliding your hand under a shirt, or crossing a collar to get to that nape of hair, that touch. But I was still stuck in girl gear then, and the thrills I got were from talking, from comfort. And with Sally it wasn't even that.

Theresa cut in for the next slow song. As soon as her mouth was within whispering distance of my ear, she said, "You look like a mink who's about to be turned into a coat."

"You've been working on that line for the past hour, haven't you?" I asked.

She nodded.

"What were some of the runner-ups?"

"Well, there was 'You look like Sylvia Plath waiting for the oven to preheat.' And 'You look like you're taking the SATs and you've only brought pens.' And just plain 'You look like a castrato.' I decided to go with the mink."

"I might've gone with Plath."

"But you haven't even read Plath."

"Maybe I'll go home right now and start."

I remember this conversation word for word. I don't remember the way I was holding Theresa or the way she was holding me. I couldn't even tell you what she was wearing. But I remember each of the things she said to me, and the way we were laughing without having the need to laugh out loud. Just sharing that.

When my dance with Theresa was over, I spied Sally talking to some of her friends at another table. The rest of my girl group—a few of them with dates in tow—joined me and Theresa as the singer tried to make her way through "Brown-Eyed Girl." At one point, I was opposite my friend Allison's date, Chad, and when we sha-la-la-la-la-la-la-la-la-le-la-dee-da-ed, we both leaned forward so that his bangs brushed up against mine. He smiled at me and I smiled back, and that was all there was. But I remember that, too.

Sally joined us—well, I should say she joined *me*—a few songs in. Some of her makeup had worn off in the sweating and her subsequent restroom visit. Her flushness came through more. The dancing scuffed up her dress, the bubble gum deflating in parts. I honestly think I was the only one who noticed.

The head of the prom committee announced the prom song, "Wonderful Tonight," and all the groups immediately split into pairs. Sally made her way into me, and I held her. Yes, I held her. Because I had been the one to ask. And because I didn't want to be an asshole. And because I knew that even if the moment didn't mean anything to me, it probably meant something to her. So I danced to the song as if it had somehow become ours. As if it showed us what we were meant to be.

When it was over, I kissed her. Closed-mouthed. Quickly. Like I would've kissed a friend on New Year's.

Further announcements were made, about not driving drunk, about remembering to take our prom memento (a coffee mug) from the table. Sally and I hadn't really talked about after the prom—I knew there were some parties, but we'd only booked the limo until midnight. Finding the limo was a nightmare—there were so many of them outside, and I barely remembered what the driver looked like. Luckily he was holding a placard with our names on it, hyphenated together. As if we were already married.

I was exhausted, and I hoped that Sally would be exhausted, too. But when we got into the limo she immediately leaned her head on my shoulder again.

"What do you want to do?" she asked, running her finger over my sleeve. I could barely feel it, but I was intensely aware of it.

"I don't know—what do you want to do?"

"How about this?" she said, leaning in closer, about to kiss me. But her dress got in her way and she didn't quite make it.

"Sally . . . ," I started.

"Damon, I'm so into you," she said. And I immediately wished she hadn't.

She was pulling her dress out of her way now, so she could push closer into me. Then her hands were on my shirt, pressing on my chest, but there really wasn't anything she could do. My sleeves were cuff-linked tight. My tuxedo buttons could only be undone from the inside. My cummerbund was safely clasped in the back, and it was protecting my pants button from any fumbling. It was like armor. And then there was her dress: Even as she rearranged the poofs, I realized there was no way for her to get out of it without some help in the back. As long as I went nowhere near her zipper, the force field would hold.

"C'mon, Damon," she whispered. "Let's make out in the back of a limo."

I'm all for making out in the back of a limo when you have a chance. But there was no way . . . except that I couldn't think of a way to tell her that.

"C'mon," she repeated, her hands getting to the back of my neck, her lips coming closer.

"I can't," I said.

She pulled back a little to look me in the eye, and asked the question I most feared:

"Why not?"

There are so many things I could have said. "I'm still in love with Nina," for one. Or that old standby "I want us just to be friends." Or "I'm not ready for another relationship." Or "I feel weird doing this with the driver of this limo sitting five feet away, with his rearview mirror aimed at us." Or "Can't we talk about this first?" Or "That would be against my God." Or, I don't know, "I have the biggest cold sore right now."

Instead I said, "Look . . . I'm gay."

It just occurred to me, and I said it, and the minute I said it, I couldn't believe I'd said it, because at that point I didn't even get it. It was like my subconscious saw an empty moment it could take for itself and went for it.

Glinda the Good Witch sagged before my eyes. She said something like "Oh, I see," and retreated into her dress, to her side of the backseat.

And I sat there on my side, thinking I had just told a lie, when it was actually the truth. I wish I could say that I suddenly realized it *was* the truth, that the minute I said it out loud it became real to me. But right then I didn't see the reasons I said it. I only see them now. I can tell you this, though—after that moment, the reasons were much harder to ignore. I thought I was making up an excuse, but it was actually the beginning of the end of excuses.

I knew none of this then, and Sally knew even less. I told her I was sorry. I asked her not to tell anyone. I said I wanted us to be friends—and that, I think, was the only real lie I told.

She didn't scream or yell or cry or anything. She just let the limo driver take her home. Who knows—maybe she actually knew more than me. Maybe the moment I said it, it made perfect sense to her.

When the limo got to her house, I told her I'd had a good time, all things considered. And in the first real moment of spark she showed the whole night, she said she'd had a good time, too, *all things considered*. I watched from the backseat as she walked up her front steps, as her mother opened the door. I felt sad for us both. And also relieved.

Of course, Theresa called the next day to ask what had happened. It wasn't until my first month of college that I started to figure things out and told her the truth.

"So the first person you came out to was Glinda the Good Witch?" she asked me. "That is *so gay*."

And I laughed, because we were okay. And I cried, because we were okay. And I thanked Sally Huston for being so wrong about me.

the escalator, a love story

When I was born, my mother loved me. That was love—
the pain and such and my head snapped into shape
by a nurse. (Of course, I'm being overdramatic. Of course
I don't remember this—I don't remember any of the times
when I was very young and everyone looked at my little body—
so chubby—and loved me instantly. Why would I want
to remember such pure love?) Certainly, my family will always
love me—it's part of the package, the unwritten pledge. But
what was my introduction to earned love? Well, I fell for
Emily Mercer in kindergarten. She had red hair, freckles,
and my heart. It didn't work out. I broke a few crayons.

Maybe I've been harmed because my best friends have been
girls—I grew up seeing both sides of love and why guys were
slime. That was always the word. Slime. So I had to prevent
myself from doing slimy things, because I wanted to be in love,
sometimes with my best friends. (Now there's a complication.)

Sure, I had crushes in elementary school. But mostly I watched,
gossiped about who would be getting valentines signed "Love,"
and who would send Love and get nothing in return.
Even in junior high—what did I know? I had an early inkling
that the boyfriend/girlfriend stuff wasn't love, just a way to fill
the space next to you. Love was long run and nothing
would ever be long run in junior high.

Now I'm in high school, wanting to fall in love
if it's not inconvenient. Do I want to be in love? Yes
and sometimes no. Do other people want me
to be in love? Hell, yes. That's why I am here now,
wandering around the mall with Mandy. Such a name, Mandy.
Not the kind poets have fun with. It's a plain name and she's
pretty plain herself. This isn't to say I don't like her. I do.
I like her, she likes me. We leave it at that. When you're in
high school, love is rare and like is enjoyable, so you just take
what you can get. And I got Mandy.

We're here in the mall, looking for a birthday present.
It's assumed we'll be giving a present together—that's what
couples are supposed to do. After a while, you become part
of a proper noun. We're Daniel-and-Mandy. It makes people
happy and jealous. I feel it, too, when I look at other couples
with something real between them. I look at their eyes, the way
they know each other's paragraphs, and something seems right.
I doubt people see that in me and Mandy, but I hope they do.
We might as well make them happy and jealous.

Mandy and I are walking through the hall, holding hands.
That's about as close as we usually get. We've kissed,

and that's about it. We don't really hang out on the fast track. Our friends say we fit, and I imagine us as Legos. My mother once told me that you really know someone when you know their parents. I think this was her way of telling me to invite Mandy over to dinner. I never have, although I guess I should. I've only been over to her house a few times. I still haven't met her father, although I think my father knows him. (I'd remark here that it's such a small world . . . but the truth is that it's just a small town.)

What do I know about love? Not much—that's the safe answer. Even when I think I have a grasp on it, something comes along to make me realize I don't know anything at all. It's just a concept to me. It's the thing that all the songs are written about, the thing that makes smart people act stupidly. If I can make love a concept, it makes me a better observer. And it also leaves a place inside of me hollow. Sometimes I can actually feel it. To reach down inside that part— I wonder how it would feel, to touch a void. That nameless empty.

This makes me seem lonely, which isn't really true. I have other parts of me—friendship, for one—which compensate for the void. I can't feel the nothingness except in those rare times when there's nothing else to feel.

Mandy must fit into a part of me. I don't feel alone as we walk from card store to card store. It feels nice to hold her hand. Not spectacular, but nice. We can't really find an interesting card. The stores are full of artificial rainbows, nicotine-voiced sarcasm that's never actually funny, and cute little cartoon animals holding Happy Birthday balloons. After making the

rounds we decide to go back upstairs to Hallmark
and give in to Snoopy and Woodstock.

There's nobody on the escalators. There's really no one in the
mall. It's February and, as my father loves to point out, we're in
a recession. Occasionally an employee will pass us, wearing a
T-shirt that says, *In My Life, I Love The Mall.* Looking at the
escalator, I have an idea. (It's actually more of an impulse than
an idea.) I turn to Mandy and say, "Why don't we go down the
up escalator?"— I used to love to do that when I was a kid, and
me and my friend Randy would be able to fit side by side and
race to the top. Running to stay still. Mandy just gives me this
what are you talking about? look that tries to convince me she
isn't in the mood. I leap onto the third or fourth stair and
start running.

The rest of the mall dissolves—I feel my legs pushing me up
against the flow. I'm making it—step, and step, and step. I
reach the final leap—the most dangerous part. Especially if your
shoelaces are untied, as mine are. I take a breath and jump onto
the second level's marble floor. I raise my arms to complete the
arc, like a champion Olympic gymnast, conqueror of the mall.

I look down and see Mandy at the base of the escalator, making
mock clapping gestures. "Come on," I yell, motioning for her
to follow. She touches her hair in hesitation. I can feel the reason
killing the impulse. "You can do it," I say, but she shrugs.
I don't understand. Anyone can do it. We're at some sort of
standstill, like when a conversation abruptly stops
and you can't think of anything more to say. I don't think
she's going to do it. I really hope she does.

I'm about to yell *"Don't bother"* with a particular edge
in my voice. But then Mandy pulls her coat firmly around her
shoulders and throws herself onto the downward escalator.
How can I explain what I suddenly feel? I see her jump,
her hair lifting in the air, and I can't help but think something
along the lines of *Wow*. I once asked Randy how he knew
that he had fallen in love with his girlfriend, Amy, and he just
looked at me like it was the hardest question in the world.
I expected some floral, florid explanation, about the air
lightening and flute music filling his ears. This relationship
that had him so transfixed—I expected a masterpiece of
sentiment, one that would make me so happy for him and
so empty inside. Instead he just turned to me and said,
"The minute I knew I was in love was the minute when
there was no question about it. One night I was lying
in the dark, looking at her looking at me, and it just
was there, undeniable."

There is no question about it. I look in amazement
as Mandy pushes herself up the stairs, not looking up
at me, concentrating on her footwork. I want so much
for her to reach the top. I want her to reach me
at this very moment. I picture myself embracing her
when she makes it, looking into her eyes for the
confirmation of my feelings. What do I feel? If it isn't
love, then it's certainly the potential for love, the realization
that there's more to us than liking and dating and being
each other's Pictionary partners. I'm so happy. I'm so
afraid. Does she feel the same way? All I know
is that I know. When she reaches the top, maybe I'll

dance with her to the piped-in non-music drifting
from the ceiling. I'll do anything—I want to do something
totally strange and new and special. I want to hold her.
I want to sleep with her—fall asleep with her in my arms.
I want to wake up that way. I've never seen her asleep.
All of these strange impulses—I want to tuck her in.
I want to be there, and be there, and be there.

And then she falls.

It's over before I can register what's happening. Her foot
hits one of the steps and, well, she trips. It isn't dramatic—
she doesn't fall down the escalator or anything.
It isn't even good comedy. She just stumbles face-first onto the
steps. Then she pushes herself up and rides the rest of the way
down. I run to her—it's as if I'm moving doubly, being
carried as I go down. I get to her. I can't tell if she's crying
or laughing. "I can't do anything!" she says, brushing back
her hair, and I see her exasperation isn't serious. I say
something along the lines of "Don't be silly, it could've
happened to anyone," and gather the things that fell
from her bag. She's still sitting when I'm done, so I offer her
my hand. She doesn't get up—she just keeps looking at me,
not at my hand but at my face. I put the bag down and sit
beside her, right there on the floor of the mall. "Are you
okay?" I ask. She says, "I fell," and I say, "I think I've fallen, too."

It's never like the movies, is it? A great romantic moment, and
clunky, corny things just tumble out. "Oh," she says, and I wonder
if she's saying it just to see what I'll offer next.

"Yeah," I reply, saying it to see what she'll say next.
Which is, "You have to be careful." Now what does that mean?
Indirect discretion. No one wants to fully commit—
everyone's afraid that they're misinterpreting because no one
is talking straight. Playing the old What Are You Thinking? game.
You have to be careful. Mandy has skinned her hands
and her lip has a little cut in one of its corners.

"Sometimes . . ." I say.

"Well . . ." she answers.

And I can't take it anymore. She just looks at me, no help at all.
But, then again, all I'm doing is looking at her. A silent standstill.
A time for something. On her lip, there's a little drop of blood.
I kiss her anyway. At this particular moment,
there's just no question about it.

THE NUMBER OF PEOPLE
WHO MEET ON AIRPLANES

This was ten years ago. I was a junior in boarding school, heading back to campus the Monday after Thanksgiving. After three rounds of leftovers, I was ready to return to the dorm, to our well-honed methodology of procrastination, to that last gasp of late-night madness before exams settled in and Christmas came.

I had planned my flight down to the last minute: I'd finish the book I was reading, proof a paper I had due, and sneak in a forty-five-minute nap before touching down in Boston. I had my head-phones to protect me from screeching children and talkative adults. I had five sharpened pencils in the front pocket of my bag. I was ready to go.

I usually liked to sit in row seventeen, because seventeen was my lucky number. This time, however, I was seated in row four-teen. I decided not to take this as a bad omen. I was not a person who normally believed in omens. Only luck.

I am always early to airports, and thus I always board when my row is first called. The overhead compartment gaped for my hand luggage. I fed all the seat pocket detritus into its maw—the shallow magazines, the safety instructions, the plastic-wrapped blanket, and the paper-clad pillow. I would keep only what was essential: my headphones, *A Room with a View*, my research paper, and three of the sharpened pencils.

As the plane filled up, I began to get hopeful; the seat next to mine was still empty, leaving me with plenty of legroom. I took up my book and started to read. I lost track of where I was, and was brought back by a tap on my shoulder. She might have said *excuse me*—I didn't hear. I looked up into the aisle. And there she was.

She was my type of pretty. Short black messabout hair, falling wherever it wanted. She was wearing a red sweater that somehow brought out that green of her eyes. She had a nice smile. I recognized this in the second before I tried to stand, even though my seat belt was already on. I continued to notice this as I unbuckled the seat belt, as she slid past me. Once she sat down and started going through the bag on her lap, I said hello.

I had never talked to a stranger on a plane before, nothing above the cursory regards. This was because I am in general an antisocial person, and because I'd never been seated next to anyone even remotely desirable. Instead I had an unerring ability to be partnered with the overweight business traveler who brought no reading material, or the father whose poor wife was across the aisle, forced to manage the demands of their children. Never anyone my own age, traveling alone. Never anyone who was my type of pretty.

She said hello back to me and scavenged deeper into her bag. I could feel my courage wavering. I tried to think of something profoundly interesting and not at all stalkeresque to say, but nothing came. I am a very strong believer in personal space, and I didn't want it to seem like I was storming hers. I was about to retreat to my headphones when she finally found what she was looking for—a copy of *A Room with a View*. The same edition as my own.

I'd always had (and still do) two rules for myself: If I were ever to pass a busker on the street who was playing the same song that was on my headphones, I would give away all the money in my wallet. And if I were ever to be riding the T and spy someone reading the same book as me, I would strike up a conversation. Again, not seeing it as an omen, but as luck.

I figured the rules of the T applied to air travel as well. Of course, I'd never actually planned what I was going to say to the person who was reading the same book as me—my thoughts had never gotten that far. So I was entirely unprepared when I looked over to her and said, "It looks like we're reading the same book."

I took mine off my lap. She looked at it, then looked at hers. She could have easily dismissed it as a little coincidence, a minor disturbance. But instead she looked back up at me and said, "Wow. Neat." Not at all sarcastic. No—she got the subtle wonder of the situation.

I knew right then that we were going to get along.

Her name was Rory. I introduced myself as Roger. She had been visiting her father for Thanksgiving, and was now going back to her mother's house in Newton, where she went to high school. We were both aiming to be English majors when we went to college, and neither one of us was reading Forster for school.

I think one of the highest compliments you can give a person is that when you are talking to her, you are not thinking about the fact that you are talking to her. That is, your thoughts and words all exist on a single, engaged level. You are being yourself because you aren't bothering to think about who you should be. It is like when you talk in a dream.

She spied my AP English research paper in the seat pocket. I ended up proofing her Virginia Woolf while she marked up my Wilfred Owen with one of her own (yes) sharpened pencils. We talked about our Thanksgivings, which really meant talking about our families in all their fragments and fissions. We began to see signs everywhere—in the fact that we'd both ordered the vegetarian meal even though neither of us was strictly vegetarian, in the fact that we were both wearing contact lenses, in the fact that we both had cousins named Jessie who were our favorites.

We talked through the in-flight movie. We talked in such a way that the flight attendants assumed we knew each other. We talked so much that we started to feel like we *did* know each other, as if every shared story could create an actual shared past.

Then the turbulence hit. I am an easy flier; I cannot tell you why, no more than I can tell you why I am afraid to climb down ladders. (Not up, just down.) From the moment the seat-belt light came back on, it was clear that Rory was *not* an easy flier. She clutched at her armrest, changed her breathing. She apologized to me and made fun of her paranoia. But I could tell that it was fear—a pure and genuine fear, the kind that rebukes rationality no matter how pleasantly or clinically the rationality is offered.

"My doctor gave me drugs, but I think I'm even more afraid of them," she told me. "He said to throw a blanket over my head and pretend I wasn't really on a plane. That was *very* helpful."

I took out her copy of my book. She was about twenty pages ahead of me, but that didn't matter. I freed her blanket from its plastic protection and threw it over both of our heads. Then, by the trail of light along my arm, I read to her. We walked around Florence as the characters courted disapproval. After a particularly sudden dip, Rory grabbed my hand without asking, and I let her without mentioning it. I kept reading, turning the pages with my one free hand as all our air turned to breath and the light of the world came in through a scrim of blue cotton. When the plane steadied off, I put the book down for a moment. Rory leaned into my shoulder with her eyes closed and a half smile on her lips. Gently, she found the right angle, the comfortable inclination. I let the book drop. I let us sleep. Two strangers under a blanket, in between two versions of home.

That is how we met. Within a few hours, we were sharing a cab even though we didn't live in the same part of town. Within a week, we were planning to meet up in Boston every chance we got. Within two months, I was sure I was in love. We dated all of senior year and decided to stay together. We went to colleges in the same city, and when we graduated, she got a job teaching in San Francisco, and I followed her there. I got a job at a family-oriented Web site just when such things were big, and left to become a teacher myself right before the Web business hit its first snag. We were married nine years to the day we met. We have become—although I'd never say this out loud—something like a model couple. The secret? We like each other. I mean, we *really* like each other. We know when to keep our space and when to share it. We are surrounded by friends—some of them dear, some of them who come with the territory.

We always loved to say *If I'd had a Monday-morning class, I never would have met you.* Or *If you'd been reading something else, none of this would have happened.* We didn't believe in fate, but we believed in serendipity. We felt very lucky.

We threw a party to mark the tenth anniversary of the day we met. We had it the Sunday after Thanksgiving, for all our friends who were returning from home, ready for a different kind of meal. Our friend Tyson brought his new boyfriend, Geoff, a flight attendant who we'd never met before. Our friend Gwen brought her boyfriend, Ted, an architect we were trying hard to like. And our friends Marcy and Will came alone, even though secretly we wished they had come together.

Both Rory and I like telling the airplane story—in no small part because it is our story, but also because we like to think it's a good story as well. Somewhere toward dessert, Ted asked us how we met. Tyson, Gwen, Marcy, and Will had heard it before, but they egged us on nonetheless. (I had been roommates with Will at the time, and he always liked to add the postscript—the look on my face as I came through the door that Monday night; even before I said a word, he knew something life-changing had occurred.) So Rory and I tag-teamed the telling—from me hoping for legroom and her hoping to catch the flight, to the discovery of the book in common, to the similar meals, oncoming turbulence, and blanket-covered reading. Of the audience, Geoff seemed to like the story the most. Perhaps because he spent his days in airplanes, perhaps because he and Tyson were newly in love.

Afterward, he and I were in the kitchen, putting the dishes into the dishwasher. It had been nice of him to volunteer—more than most of Tyson's previous boyfriends had done. I was sure Rory was pointing this out to Tyson, somewhere in the other room.

"That's so funny, what you said about your lucky row," Geoff said to me. "I know this is going to sound strange, but didn't you say you'd requested row seventeen?"

I nodded. "I did. But when I checked in, it was switched. They probably made a mistake. A very lucky mistake, as far as I'm concerned."

"And what airline was it?"

I told him the airline.

"And what airport did you leave from?"

I told him the airport.

"Hmmm . . ."

He'd stopped drying now and was just looking at me, doing some mental math.

"What?" I asked.

"Oh, this is crazy. It was ten years ago, you said?"

"Almost to the day."

"Okay—now I'm going to ask you a *really* strange question. Do you by any chance remember what the man behind the ticket counter looked like when you checked in?"

"No. I'm not even sure it was a man. Why?"

Geoff's eyes gleamed. He took the towel out of my hand and tilted his head to one of our kitchen chairs. "You'd better sit down a sec," he said, "and let me tell you about Al Schwartz."

Al Schwartz was a legend in airline circles. He wasn't a pilot or a flight attendant. He wasn't in management or a leader of one of the unions. No, for almost forty years he worked the ticket counter, without once missing a day of work. He was the Cal Ripken of airline employees. But even more than that—he was a famed matchmaker.

He didn't do it often, but when he did, legend said that he almost always got it right. It worked like this: An unmarried person would arrive to check in for his flight. If he was already booked between two people and Schwartz had an instinct about him, he would be switched to a new row with an available seat next to his. Then a second unmarried person would check in. If Schwartz felt strongly that this person would get along with the first person, he would seat her in that available seat. The rest would be up to them.

At first, he did this in secret, not telling a soul. (It was rightly believed that supervisors wouldn't take too kindly to this meddling; it was something short of a flight attendant flirting with a passenger, but it still smacked of impropriety.) After many years, however, word got out. Pilots and flight attendants leaving from Schwartz's airport would wonder if their flights had been graced with prospective lovebirds. Bets would be made; results would be tallied. Schwartz denied everything and kept doing all he could. When his colleagues would ask him to set them up, he'd always shake his head. He only made matches when the people involved had no idea.

"But where is he now? How can I find out if he had anything to do with Rory and me?" I asked Geoff.

"He retired a while ago," he told me. "But don't you worry—I'm sure I can track him down. Consider it my anniversary present."

Two weeks later I got a postcard from Paris. On the back, Geoff had scribbled an address in Nevada, adding *No phone* with two underlines and *Good luck!* with three.

I didn't tell Rory. I know I should have, but part of me liked having this secret, wanted to be able to present her with the full story. So I kept the postcard hidden in my desk and pondered the letter I knew I had to write.

I was out of practice. I hadn't written a true letter in an embarrassing number of years. I communicated with my friends through e-mail, and didn't really communicate with anyone else besides my friends. I knew writing Schwartz wasn't something I could just toss off. I knew it was something I had to do by hand.

I waited until the quietest moment possible to write. I will not recount my drafts (or even count them), but will simply say that this is what I ended up with:

Dear Mr. Schwartz,

My wife and I met on [here I gave our airline and flight number] from [the airport] on [the date]. A friend just brought it to my attention that you might have had something to do with this. I was supposed to be in the seventeenth row, but was switched at check-in to seat 14B. If you had nothing to do with this, I apologize for taking up your time. If you did in fact seat my wife (her name is Rory Wright) and me together on that day, I would appreciate it if you could respond to the address below. Either way, I thank you.

Sincerely,
Roger Lewis

Ten days later, I received this response on a clean white notecard:

Dear Mr. Lewis,

I do believe I may have had something to do with it, although I hasten to add that you and your wife had the most to do with it. I await your visit with pleasure.

Fly high,
Al Schwartz

My visit? At first thought, it seemed ludicrous. But over the next few minutes, a plan took form. Las Vegas was not so far away from San Francisco; I could be there and back in a single sick day. If Mr. Schwartz had indeed made a match of me and Rory, the least I could do was visit and hear his story. I owed it to him. And I owed it to my curiosity, which (to be honest) rarely got out of the house.

I sent a letter to tell him when I was coming. I stopped short of giving him the flight information.

Ten days later I was in a rent-a-car wrestling with a map of Nevada. In truth, I didn't have far to go. He lived five minutes from the airport.

I was early, so I drove around the flat-top neighborhood for a little while, trying not to get lost among the cookie-cutter condos. After about fifteen minutes, I spied a man in his front yard waving me down.

This, I was soon to discover, was Al Schwartz.

"Are you Mr. Lewis?" he asked once I'd pulled over.

"Yes. Mr. Schwartz?"

"Yes, sir. Now get on out of the car. The neighbors are starting to get nervous, seeing a strange car drive around and all."

Mr. Schwartz was eighty if a day, with thick white hair that made him seem tanner than he really was. He was shorter than me, although he might have once been the same height. He walked now with a bit of a stoop, but it didn't seem to slow him down. He was wearing an old cardigan over what could only be a pajama top, the broad soft collar reaching floppily for each shoulder.

"This way, Mr. Lewis," he said, leading me to the front door.

"Call me Roger," I told him.

He nodded. "Can do, Roger. But I hope you don't mind if I stick with Mr. Schwartz. That's what most of my friends call me, anyway."

The house was modest on the outside; inside, it bragged. Paintings of airplanes and photographs of people fought for position against newspapers and knickknacks. The photographs showed all the younger versions of Mr. Schwartz, in work uniform and in the various guises of vacation uniform—Hawaiian shirts with matching colored cocktails, hiking gear to face the distant snowcapped mountains, black tie for a bygone nightclub. The same woman was with him in most of the photos. Her clothes and her body altered, but her hair never changed its color.

"That's Mrs. Schwartz," he said proudly. "She was one helluva gal. She passed three years ago. But we had great times. Real great times." He held up his finger and showed me his wedding ring, then pulled at a thin chain around his neck to reveal another ring—hers—that he kept under his clothes.

"One for my hand, one for my heart," he explained. There was both sorrow and pride in his voice.

He led me into a sitting room that was as cluttered as the hall. There were more photos covering the walls—some in frames, some cornered with Scotch tape.

"She'd kill me if she saw what I did to her wallpaper. But if you have photos, you should look at them, right?" He motioned for me to sit down on the lime-green couch while he lowered himself into a lounge chair surrounded by a moat of discarded newspapers and magazines. "But you didn't come all this way for decorating tips, did you?"

I was staring at him, trying to remember that brief moment ten years ago. How long does it take to check in for a flight? Two minutes? So I was trying to recapture two minutes that happened over five million minutes ago. Which would seem ridiculous, if only I didn't recall so many other things from that day. All of them leading to Rory.

"I'm trying to remember," I told him, explaining my silence and my stare.

He nodded. "Seems reasonable. But I have to tell you, not many people remember. Even the most friendly people, the ones you really strike up a conversation with—our minds don't want them to take up the space. So we forget. I've had a few remember, but mostly those are people who were tipped off or who retraced their steps soon after. How long did you say it was?"

"Ten years."

He brushed the figure aside with a wave of his hand. "Well, come on then. Ten years is a long time for you. For me, it's yesterday. But for you, it's everything."

He asked me if I wanted something to drink. I said water would be great. He told me he made sure to have six glasses of water a day, which (he said) was probably why he was still around to talk to me.

While he went to the kitchen, I looked around the room some more. By my feet, there was a long wooden coffee table covered with more framed photos, maybe two dozen or so. These, however, weren't of Mr. and Mrs. Schwartz. They were of weddings and babies, or of babies grown up into kids. Black kids, Asian kids, white kids. An assemblage of smiles and poses, some with Woolworth backdrops and some in backyards and bedrooms.

Behind me, Mr. Schwartz said, "My children. From all across the world. All different mothers, and I was never unfaithful to Mrs. Schwartz. Quite a trick, no?"

"How did it start?" I asked.

Mr. Schwartz handed me a glass of water and sat down. He made himself comfortable in the chair and leaned over to me. "You're not going to believe this, but flying used to be quite romantic. To fly—people couldn't believe it. You only get that in little kids now. But back at the start, there was this sense of the future about flying. You were buying a ticket to this experience, this wonderful thing. Sure, people were nervous then. But that made it even more exciting. There was this expectation that something thrilling would happen, that being off the ground could take you out of your world for a few hours. I felt that way the first times I flew. I was already married to Margie then, but every liftoff—for fifty years—we would hold hands when we took to the air. Not out of fear. Out of wonder.

"I'd see it in people's eyes when they came to me for their seats, with their tickets and their luggage. I never intended to do what I ended up doing. But there was this one time, this man—a real friendly guy, and clearly a brain, too—he told me he had flown dozens of times, but it was always like the first. I liked him, in the way you can like someone after talking to him for a minute. We struck up a conversation and he mentioned he wasn't married, and I thought, *Well, that's a pity*. He leaves, and maybe two minutes later this young woman—about his age—comes up. A looker, but not real aware of it. Her hand is shaking a little when she hands over her ticket, and I can tell she's a little nervous. She's very sweet and I can see she isn't wearing any wedding ring. Miss Jane Halstead, her ticket says. She has the luggage of a society girl, but she doesn't carry herself that way. So I don't know where it comes from, but I get to thinking—what would happen if I sat Miss Jane Halstead next to the man I'd just been talking to? No harm done if nothing comes of it. And maybe, just maybe, they'll strike up a conversation and he'll help her be less nervous about the flight. That's all I was thinking. Nothing beyond that.

"So I changed her seat and sent her on her way. Wouldn't have thought anything of it. But then, not three months later, I see that name again—Miss Jane Halstead. And this time it's in the paper, in the wedding announcements. I look at the photo, and sure as I'm sitting here, I see her all decked out, standing next to the guy from the plane. Mrs. Schwartz and I had a laugh about that, I tell you. Then the same situation came up again. And again. Sometimes the man's nervous. Sometimes it's the woman. Sometimes they're both okay with it, but I see that's not all. People want to be together.

"It's the story of life, I tell you—you do something small, and it just gets bigger. Now, don't get me wrong—a lot of the times I matched people up, it probably didn't hold. It's not like I kept score. Probably have an average that would get me kicked out of the minors. But every now and then, there'd be something in the paper. Or word would get back. People would find out and would find me."

"Like me," I said.

"Well, that remains to be seen."

"Geoff, the flight attendant who told me about you, said you were a kind of legend."

"Pshaw," Mr. Schwartz exhaled dismissively. "I was probably just trying to jazz up my job during slow periods. I really did love it, though. Not this matchmaking business, but being behind the counter, talking to people. I mean, I met hundreds, if not *thousands*, of people each day. Sometimes it would kick the stuffing out of me. But most of the time I could come home to Mrs. Schwartz with a story or two to tell. You can't ask for much more than that—a good woman and a story to tell."

"I know what you mean."

A nod. "I'm glad that you do. So many don't. I was starting to get sad. This was before Mrs. Schwartz passed. The job was getting to me. I didn't want to admit it, but the lifting was shooting my back to hell. Knees, too. And the people had changed. Everyone was in a rush. Everyone. I was something getting in their way. Margie could see this better than I could. People don't know how to fly. It's something that was once magical, but now we're afraid of it."

I thought, at that moment, of Rory. I thought about how she didn't know where I was at this moment, and how it would drive her crazy if she knew she didn't know. If she called and I wasn't there. If we were that kind of apart.

"So tell me why you're here," Mr. Schwartz continued, after taking a sip from his glass of water. He leaned forward in his chair and said, "Give me the details."

So I told him the story—our story—the story of how we met. I started with my family's Thanksgiving and my lucky number seventeen. I told him everything I could remember, from the red sweater and the green eyes to the passage of Forster to which I had briefly turned. He didn't say a word, just took it all in.

After I had finished—after Rory and I had taken the cab home together, after Rory and I had said our first "I love you," after we'd been married and had created our ongoing life—this old man in front of me, this matchmaker of the skies, nodded and asked me if I still had the boarding pass.

Of course I had the boarding pass. I had kept it as a permanent bookmark in my copy of *A Room with a View*, just as Rory (unbeknownst to me until the first time I saw her apartment) had done with hers. Now the two books sat side by side in our bedroom, our most prized possessions.

Under Al Schwartz's expectant gaze, I reached into my bag. For the first time in ten years, I separated the boarding pass from the book. As I handed it over, he reached under his sweater, into his pajama-top pocket for his reading glasses. It only took him a second's glance to know.

He took off his glasses and looked at me straight before speaking.

"I know I wrote this in my letter to you, but I must repeat it now: After all is said and done, you have to remember that it was you and your wife who made all of this possible. I may have been the one to sit you next to each other—in fact, I'm sure I did. But you took it from there. I have nothing to do with all that."

"So it was you behind the counter?" I asked. I was no longer surprised by this turn of events; I hadn't been, really, since we'd started talking. "How do you know?"

He handed the boarding pass back to me. "Look at the seat assignment. What do you see?"

I looked down. "It's circled in green," I said.

"Aha. Look again. Is it really circled?"

I looked again. The green pen, rounding around the number. A circle. Only . . .

"It's an 'a'?" I asked.

Mr. Schwartz smiled. "You've cracked it."

"It's a green 'a,' " I said, clear now.

"That's what I'd do. I used the green for everything, but only the people I thought might be right for each other got the 'a.' I'm amazed nobody picked up on it; they all thought it would be a color thing, or I'd initial it somewhere else. Do you have your wife's pass?"

I nodded, then took it out. Sure enough—another "a."

"That's amazing," I said.

Mr. Schwartz laughed. "Actually," he said, "it's not amazing at all. Or at least my part of it isn't."

"But all along we thought it was random." Chance. Luck.

Mr. Schwartz looked serious now. "But it *was* random, can't you see? I need you to see that. Why did you arrive at the counter before her? There were at least five check-in windows at that airport for our airline—how did the two of you both end up at mine? Love weaves itself from hundreds of threads. Happenstances. I just happened to be one of them."

"An important one."

"Yes, I'll grant you that. But not the most important. Not by a long shot. You're together because you spoke to each other . . . because you *liked* each other. That's the greatest leap of all. I didn't push you. I didn't even give you a nudge. I just created the nearness and you did the rest."

It still felt different. How could I describe it to him? I still felt lucky . . . but now I had someone to thank for the luck.

"Anyway," he added, "if the two of you hadn't been nice to me at the ticket counter, I never would've given you the 'a'!"

He stood up from his chair, and I immediately sensed our time together would soon be over. Gratitude is not something that should impose itself, so I stood, too.

"I'm a lucky man," Mr. Schwartz said, putting his hand on my arm. "One of my old pals from the airline is the boss out at the airport here, and he lets me walk around sometimes, talking to people. And, believe me, I've heard stories of other ticket counter personnel finding out about what I did and trying it out themselves. You'd be surprised, I tell you, the number of people who meet on airplanes."

I thanked him for seeing me, and then tried to thank him for what he'd done ten years before.

"It was—and still is—my pleasure," he interrupted. "Say no more. Just drop me a line every now and again. Bring your wife by if you're ever in the neighborhood."

I promised I would. We made a little more small talk as he walked me to the door. We said our good-byes, and then, just as I was walking through the door, Al Schwartz asked me one more question.

"Just out of curiosity," he said, resting his hand on a photo of his wife, "did you change your lucky number?"

"No," I told him. "It's still seventeen."

"Good," he replied, visibly pleased. "You should *never* change your lucky number."

I made in onto an earlier flight home. At the ticket counter, I was sure to be friendly, and sure to show my wedding ring. I got to our house a little later than I would have from school. Rory's car was in the driveway. When I got inside, I called out to her. She called back from the kitchen, saying she was on the phone.

I put my bag down, home for the day, and went to where she was. She smiled when she saw me, then went back to talking to a fellow teacher about faculty-room gossip. The phone must have rung as soon as she got in the house. Her shoes were off, but they were still at her feet. She kicked them lightly as she talked. She took off her earrings.

I felt love. Right there, in the kitchen. And I felt relief.

Because a part of me had worried that the truth would somehow change things. But now I saw her and knew that nothing had changed. Nothing would change. Only the story would change.

When she was off the phone, I was going to tell her about the beginning we'd never known we'd had.

I was going to tell her a story of how we met.

ANDREW CHANG

I guess I'll start with this fact: I still to this day have no idea what my father does for a living. I'm sure he and my mother would say that this is a failure on my part. My brother would know, because they would tell him and not me. When I was a kid, I was told that my father was in "import/export." From what I could tell, the only thing he exported were long-distance phone calls, and the only thing he imported were business partners.

The only way I could tell the difference between the business partners in China and the business partners in America was the amount of static on the phone when they called. And they called almost every hour of the day. Every time I used the phone, my parents looked at me like I was jeopardizing the family business. Whenever the call waiting beeped, I knew I'd have to get off the line. Because it was always Mr. Chen or Mr. Yang or Mr. Wei or some other monosyllabic partner. They never acknowledged my existence—they simply said my father's name and held there until I got him.

It bothered me without ever interesting me. I would complain to my brother, and he would tell me that there were worse things to suffer than call interruption. He was a year older than me and reading Camus at that point. He had promised my father he'd go to business school, and that was all he needed to get a free pass for the rest of his senior year.

My life and my father's business would have never intersected, except one night at dinner my father made an offhand comment about Mr. Chang having a son named Andrew who lived three towns over.

"He is your age," my father said, and the way he said it—as if this was a sign of some kind—made the alarms go off in my head.

"I don't know him," I said. "Hey, did I tell you we're going to Philadelphia on a field trip?"

My brother smiled snidely as my mother picked up my father's conversational thread.

"You should meet him," she said. "You could be friends."

This was particularly special coming from a woman who didn't seem to believe that any boy I knew could be anything other than a sex-starved boyfriend. Every time one of my male friends called—especially the white ones—she would look concerned, as if a phone call was one short step away from impregnation.

For some reason, I felt that if I simply ignored my parents, the topic would go away, even though there was no evidence of this ever having worked in the sixteen previous years of my life. I started chattering about the Liberty Bell and Independence Hall. My brother continued to smirk and my parents waited me out, gazing at me attentively, knowing I had steered myself onto a tangent that could only last for so long.

Right after I dropped the big news that we'd be riding commuter buses instead of school buses on our field trip, I quickly asked, "Can I be excused?"

In answer, my mother said, "He really is a startling boy."

Startling could not have been the word she meant to use; I knew that. Still, it startled me into temporary submission. If she'd said *nice* or *intelligent*, I probably would have found the strength to get up from the table and leave.

"We would like you to meet him," my father said. "The Friday after next."

"I can't," I told him.

"Why not?" my mother asked.

"I'm busy," I said, sure that I could find a way to be busy with a week and a half's notice.

My mother stood up and walked to the refrigerator door, where she kept a calendar of her two children's activities.

"With what?" she asked. "I checked. You are free."

"Fine," I said. "Fine." It took too much strength to argue, and I needed some pluses in my column for future minus situations.

Both of my parents smiled—and, believe me, that was something very rare for my father.

I clung to the hope that it was just a friend thing.

Until, of course, I realized my brother hadn't been invited along.

I didn't think much about it. My mother fussed over me in a nicer way than she usually did, and I figured I could definitely use a week and a half of that. When I told my friends about it, I told the story like it was a joke that was waiting for its punch line. I'd already dated a guy named Andrew, so whenever I talked about my date-to-be, I called him Andrew Chang or, sometimes, Mr. Chang's Son.

Two days before I was supposed to meet him, my mother appeared in my doorway with a garment bag. Since my parents had an open-door policy regarding my room—it was only closed when I was asleep—she didn't knock or even clear her voice to let me know she was there. She just stood in the doorway for a minute until I looked up from my homework and saw her.

"I have something for you to wear," she said.

I can't think of another time that my mother went out and bought me clothes. No, it was important to her to drag me along whenever my clothing was purchased, so she could show me the correct way to shop for and purchase it. It wasn't fashion she was after, but education. Even at that moment, she couldn't hand the garment bag over and let me open it as if it were a gift. No, instead she unzipped it herself, pulling out an astonishing blue dress and holding it out in front of me without a word of presentation.

It looked like an ocean—it was that kind of blue. And although the neckline was bordering on a turtle's, it was sleeveless—something I couldn't have imagined my mother buying for me before. It was a party dress, a fancy dress. My first thought was that my father had won some kind of award, and that there was going to be a dinner in his honor. I in no way related it to my upcoming encounter with Mr. Chang's Son until my mother said, "I am sure Andrew will like it."

"What kind of date is this?" I asked her.

She smiled knowingly. "A special one."

I was going to protest, but here's the thing: I really liked the dress. So I kept my mouth shut. I figured I'd already said I was going. I might as well get a dress out of it. And this dress wasn't cheap.

Later that night my brother came into my room and saw it hanging from the top of my closet door.

"I can't believe you're letting them arrange your marriage," he said.

"Don't you have business school applications to fill out?" I replied.

He looked at me for a moment like I was the stupidest girl in the world, then said, "Have it your way."

What I wouldn't admit to him—what I would've *never* admitted to my parents—was that there was a small part of me that actually wanted it to work out. I was already burning out on high school dating, on making poorly educated guesses and committing myself to other people's commitment issues. Perhaps, I figured, this was the way to do it: no anxiety, no flirting, no friends involved, no falling. Just a simple agreement. It didn't even occur to me to call or IM or e-mail Andrew Chang and communicate with him before our date. It didn't even occur to me to ask my parents more about him. I was playing by a certain set of rules, and I obeyed because the rules didn't ask me to do anything. I simply had to wait. And then, when the day came, I had to make it work.

My mother told me to come straight home after school on Friday. The minute I walked through the door, she pointed me to the shower. When I got out, towel-wrapped and a little tired, she did something she hadn't done in ages. She sat me down at her makeup mirror and she brushed out my hair. It hurt—there were knots in there that had been tangled for semesters. But she was persistent, and before I knew it the brush was running smoothly through my hair.

At the end, my mother put down the brush, looked at my reflection in the mirror, and said, satisfied, "There."

I put on the dress. It made me feel grown up, like my own older sister.

As I was finishing up, I heard the garage door open. I figured it was my brother, but instead my father came up from the basement. I heard him ask my mother, "Is she ready?" I did not hear my mother's reply.

I figured Mr. Chang's Son was taking me to a nice restaurant, trying to impress my parents. And I figured my mother had gone a little overboard dressing me up, trying to impress *his* parents. But when Andrew Chang arrived at five-thirty in a limousine, I started to think that maybe things were going a little too far.

"What does Mr. Chang do?" I asked my mother after peeking out the window at the black stretch Cadillac. "Is that his car?"

The back door opened and nobody got out. I suddenly imagined a three-hundred-pound boy in the backseat, waiting for me. About thirty seconds passed before Andrew Chang realized he had to come out and get me. He emerged from the back door wearing a tuxedo, looking much cuter than I had any right to expect. He got to our front door and rang the doorbell.

My mother went to get it, me trailing behind. My father took out his camera.

I think my mother expected me to wait in the living room, because she seemed surprised to see me in the foyer when she ushered Andrew Chang inside.

"Here she is," she said.

"Hello," I said.

"Hello," Andrew Chang replied. "Should we go?"

He was a little taller than I was, but not by much. He looked handsome, but I couldn't tell whether that was all the tux's doing.

He didn't seem uncomfortable with the situation, but he didn't seem to be welcoming it, either.

My parents didn't notice. They had us pose for some pictures before they let us leave. My mother was all smiles, my father all nods. Mr. Chang called my father to make sure Andrew had made it. In his loud business voice, my father said Andrew was here and that I looked good. I blushed, but Andrew seemed unfazed.

He had left the limo's back door open, so he didn't have to open it for me. Again, I was thinking it was all a little too much, but I also enjoyed the idea of telling my friends that a date had picked me up in a limo.

When I got to the backseat, it all started to kick in. There was a corsage waiting for me.

A corsage.

Andrew Chang joined me in the backseat, and as soon as he closed the door, the driver took us away from my house.

"Andrew?" I asked. "What's that?"

"For you," he said. "My mother picked it out. Your mother told her what you were wearing."

"But where are we going?"

"To the prom."

From his tone, I couldn't tell whether he expected that I already knew this or whether he was aware that it was news to me.

"Your *prom*?"

"Yes. Do you like the flowers? My mother picked them out."

"Andrew," I said, remembering to keep his last name out of it, "I had no idea we were going to a prom. I thought this was a date. I mean, dinner. Friendship. That kind of thing."

"Oh," he said, looking out the window. "It's a prom."

I knew immediately that there was nothing I could do about it.

I couldn't ask him to pull over the car or turn around. I couldn't get out of it. If I went to my parents to complain, they'd find a way to turn it back on me—I hadn't asked them if it was a prom, had I? They'd never said it wasn't a prom, right? I was too stunned to cry and not detached enough to laugh. I couldn't even speak, and he showed no inclination to speak. So we sat there in awkward silence until we got to his prom.

I know this will sound strange, but after a short while, Andrew Chang and Mr. Chang started to blend in my head. I don't even know if I'd ever met Mr. Chang. I just had this idea of him as one of my father's generic business partners—hair slicked back, comb marks visible; an expensive suit that looked average; no enthusiasm for anything but talk of business; a scowl across his face while he thought of new ways to make money. I'm sure there was more to him than that—more to all of them—but from my daughter perspective, that's all they were. And Andrew Chang was like that, too. Younger, yes. But younger in body, not in spirit.

We sat at our table. He was polite, getting me a soda, pulling my chair out for me when I sat down, then pushing it in. I tried to make conversation. I asked him how long he'd lived in Fairview. He said three months. I figured that was why he didn't seem to know anyone else at our table, or in the whole room. The other girls at the table were nice enough, complimenting me on my dress, asking me where I was from. But the guys didn't seem to have anything to say to Andrew, and he didn't seem to have anything to say, either. When the table cleared out to go to the dance floor, he stayed seated. I stayed seated next to him. I watched the dance floor. He stared off somewhere.

Finally, he said, "You can dance if you want to. I'll be here."

He had no idea how ludicrous this was. There was no way I was going to dance alone with a school of strangers.

I compromised and said I would step out to the ladies' room for a moment. He nodded. I fled.

I didn't even have to go, but I ended up in the ladies' room anyway. I stood in front of the mirror and realized I did in fact look good. And that it really didn't matter. I washed my hands. I looked at myself again. I tried to stay there as long as I could.

Girls came and went behind me, beside me. One girl, drunk, put her hand on my shoulder and asked, "Who are you?"

"I'm Andrew Chang's date," I said.

She nodded, swerved away, then swerved back.

"Who's he?" she asked.

"Friend of the family."

She nodded again. I wanted her to stay, to ask me something else. But she left to be with her friends.

I returned to the prom but hung in the back, against the wall. It was strange to be watching all these people I didn't know. At first, I felt like an observer. But gradually it didn't even feel that interesting. I understood for the first time what the term *wallflower* meant. Because that was what I was. Just hanging there. Nobody noticing. Useless decoration.

I looked at our table and saw Andrew Chang sitting there alone. I didn't know whether he was simply hiding his misery or if he was somehow able to close himself off from it. He looked like this was work, that this was just something he had to do. I felt sorry for him . . . but mostly I felt mad that I had been trapped, too.

A guy from our table walked by me, on the way to the men's room. We'd all exchanged names at the beginning, but I'd already forgotten them. He walked past on the way in, but on the way back he stopped at my spot on the wall and asked me how I was doing.

"Fine," I said.

He laughed and said, "Yeah, right."

I concentrated on him then. He was Chinese, too, taller than my date, all of his features narrower. His hair wasn't a comb job—there was definitely some spiking going on.

"Do you want to know the truth?" I asked. He said yes, and I told it to him. The whole story.

"Well," he said when I was through, "all I can say is that right now my date is dancing with her boyfriend." And he told me his story, about how he'd asked this girl as a friend, and then two weeks ago she'd started dating this guy he didn't particularly like. She wasn't going to bail on the prom plans, but of course the minute she got to the dance, she wanted to be with her real boyfriend. So he let her. He'd danced with a few of his friends who'd also wanted to abscond from their dates, and now he was here with me.

"Do you want to dance?" he asked.

And I said yes.

I went to the table and asked Andrew if he minded. He said no. I told him to watch my purse. And then I absconded.

The new guy couldn't dance to save his life. I mean, he couldn't move his feet and his arms at the same time. But still, he kept drawing me into the dance, including me. And then when the prom song was played, he asked me with the sweetest expression if I would stay. We didn't do much more than sway there, his arms around me, my arms around him. But I found myself thinking, *It can't be this easy.*

When the fast dancing started again, I flailed along with him. The flower who fell from the wall.

He couldn't dance, but he could make me laugh, and he could make me happy.

And he still makes me laugh. And he still makes me happy.

I have no idea what happened to Andrew Chang.

FLIRTING WITH WAITERS

I have always flirted with waiters. I think it was my parents who first encouraged this—when I was a little girl, they loved it when I acted cute for the waitstaff. Winsomeness made them proud. I know most parents do this, and I know that in some girls it wears off well before puberty sets in. But for me it never wore off. For me it's still a thrill.

I did, however, narrow my scope. First I lost interest in the younger waitresses, the ones who took orders between chews of gum, who wanted the jobs so they could flirt with the boys who came in. They had no use for girls like me. Next to go were the older men—the waiters like butlers, the ones as old as the oldest wine on the wine list. Most were too grandfatherly, and the ones who weren't grandfatherly were just wolves with flimsy teeth. While I never lost respect for older waitresses—I still love being called *darlin'* and *hon*—I knew I could never be anything more than a sob sister with them, our intimacy limited to knowing looks, pats on the shoulder, and comfort food.

That left the boys, the guys, the young waiters and their marvelous eyes, their hair grown long, their nonchalant way of pleasing, their rebellious asides, their erogenous hands, their clean white shirts and black ties, often a little askew. I knew early on that resistance wouldn't work. I was destined to flirt with these waiters.

Let me be clear here—it wasn't sex, or even love, that I was after. Before I was twelve, I didn't figure there was anything more exciting than a spark of recognition, a moment of reciprocal attention.

Then came the pizza boy.

He was not technically a waiter, at least not at first. He drove a green VW—*his own car*—and when he was working he'd put a little sign on the top that said LA ROTA PIZZERIA. He was, in my twelve-year-old eyes, a dream on legs. Lithe, fair-skinned, with hair that fell in a curtain over his face. His name was Seth and I could think of no better name.

My parents both worked. Sometimes they wouldn't make it home for dinner, especially once I was old enough to take care of myself. (I am an only child.) That year no words were more beautiful to me than *Take some money from the drawer and call for something*. Seth's shift ended at eight, so I would run to the phone as early as possible to place my order. Sometimes my friend Bev would come over to watch as Seth walked the fourteen steps up to my door, rang the bell, and talked to me like an adult for the minute or two it took to receive the pizza and pay him for it. I always ordered the same thing: one small pizza, half mushroom and half plain. After a few visits he noticed this, and when he handed over the pizza he would call it *the usual*. I thought this was our own private joke, like the ones couples in high school had.

I did not have the courage to flirt with him yet. Not at twelve, my period year, with my breasts not catching up as much as I thought they should and my body sensitive to every change of wind. It was enough for me to admire. It was enough for me to have Seth come to *my house* in *his own car* and say "the usual" with a smile. (Dimples!) I always tipped really well, and would have done so even if it had been my own money.

Then one day I called and a girl came. She didn't know my usual, and since she was a girl—a *high school girl*—I didn't dare ask about Seth. What if she was somehow responsible for his absence? It was Bev who broke the news to me two nights later: she and her dad had gone to La Rota to eat in, and there was Seth . . . doing table service. I knew I had to take action. If he would not come to me, I would go to him.

Bev was a more-than-willing accomplice. (Luckily I had announced my crush first, so I had dibs.) After school—that station between Seth sightings—we would head over to the pizzeria. We had to take a little time, since Seth wouldn't come to work until his lacrosse practice was over. If there was a game, we'd dare to hit the stands and watch, careful to sit in the family rows, safe from the girlfriends. I wondered which girlfriend was Seth's (I was jaded enough to know he was bound to have one). To my extreme distress, it ended up being the delivery girl—I knew her name was Sheryl because she had it stitched on her varsity soccer jacket.

At first it was strange—almost a shock—to see Seth in his red-vested uniform at the restaurant. Then I adapted it into my admiration: If he could look hot in a red-and-white striped shirt—an ironed barbershop pole—he could look hot in just about anything.

If you asked me now what the high point of my childhood was, it wouldn't be my Bat Mitzvah or my time at summer camp or any cherished moment I spent with my grandmother or a horse. No, it would be the first time I slid into a seat at La Rota and Seth came over, order pad in hand. Smiling at me, he asked, "The usual?"

I used up most of my allowance on small pizzas and Diet Cokes. I no longer dressed for school—I dressed for *after* school. My parents worried that I had an eating disorder because I ate so little at dinner. I couldn't tell them that I'd just had a pizza a couple of hours before, so instead I told them I was a vegetarian, ate lighter dinners, and sacrificed lunch when I felt I could.

Second highlight of my childhood: When Seth asked my name. Granted, he asked Bev's name, too (I still couldn't go to the pizza place alone; that was too weird). But Bev couldn't look up when he talked to her, and I could. This, to me, was the beginning of flirting.

It would have been paradise if Sheryl hadn't been around, coming in after each delivery, waiting for a noisy welcome-back kiss. (She was the only one making a noise, I noted.) She stopped wearing her varsity jacket and starting wearing his. I couldn't see what she gave him in return.

After a couple of months passed, he would sometimes sit down with us, ask us which teachers we had, give us some advice on making it through junior high. (Sheryl was never around for this.) One time he asked me (*not* Bev) if I had a boyfriend, and I thought I was going to die right there. It had never, ever occurred to me that he would ask this question. I was dumbstruck. If I said no, I'd sound like a loser who couldn't even manage to have a boyfriend in eighth grade. If I said yes, I'd be . . . unavailable. So I did the stupidest thing imaginable. I said *maybe*. And it worked. Seth smiled and said, "How *mysterious*."

Something inside me—the woman I would one day become—knew to smile back. Mysteriously.

The true hardships came in March. Sheryl started wearing a pretty necklace that could've possibly been given to her by Seth. Bev had play practice three times a week after school. Hal, the owner of La Rota, starting hassling Seth about which college he'd choose. And my mother got off work early one Thursday, looked into La Rota's window on her way to a manicure, and saw Bev and me eating a greasy slice an hour before I was supposed to be home for dinner.

My mother's discovery was the most pressing problem—burgeoning flirt though I was, I knew I didn't have the courage to rebel if my parents forbade me to get pizza in the afternoon. Under no circumstances could I tell my mother what Bev and I had really been doing there, so I searched for the easiest available lie and blamed it all on Bev's parents' divorce. Bev, I said, was having a hard time. She was feeling very vulnerable and didn't want to eat alone. Her mother and father meant well, but sometimes they would have to work late (I knew to tread carefully here) and Bev had been skipping dinner instead of eating in her empty house. So the afternoon pizza was my mission of mercy. My mother, who knew enough about her divorced friends to know this was plausible, told me I had done the right thing, and paid me back for that Thursday's excursion.

Sheryl decided to go to Florida State and then Seth decided to go to Northwestern, which really (it was so clear) pissed her off. He was free now—into college, second-semester senior (which, from what I could tell, was like being in kindergarten all over again, for all the responsibility he had). But he didn't look happy. And he didn't look I'm-going-to-miss-Sheryl-so-much sad. Something sadder than that.

He didn't stop sitting at my table, even on those days when Bev was busy and it was just him and me and a slowly sipped soda.

By May he was asking me which teachers I'd have next year, even though I didn't know yet. With other customers, he always seemed to be searching for something to say. Sheryl would still come in and they'd still kiss, but like me with my half-mushroom, half-plain pizza—*the usual*—Seth seemed to have grown tired of it.

I became a little more forthcoming. I complimented him on his shirts, which were now branching out from the red and white stripes. I even went so far as to say one of them really brought out the green of his eyes. He said thank you but didn't take the compliment with him when he left. I could tell. I congratulated him when a lacrosse game went well, and he seemed genuinely touched that I'd been in the stands. He started slipping me free Diet Cokes. I left him drawings folded in napkins.

My mood about the whole thing swung wildly. Sometimes I'd think I was just this eighth-grade pain in the ass, this little sister, this *pest*. But then I'd be talking to Bev and we'd have it all planned out. We'd get Seth to break up with Sheryl. He'd take all of college to recover from it. If he brought home a girlfriend from Northwestern, we'd break them up, too. After college, when he moved back to our town, his heartbreak would be old enough to have healed. I would be a second-semester senior. He'd see me and realize I'd always been there for him, that I was everything he'd been looking for in all of the others, that I was his true chance at love.

Bev invited him to her play, but he couldn't make it. I showed him my ninth-grade schedule when it came, and he gave me all the dirt. Lacrosse season was now over. Soon school would be over, too, and we'd be in that magic hour between classes and summer. Hal announced that he was throwing Seth a graduation party, and seemed pleased when Seth invited us. We were happy beyond words. We had no idea what we'd wear, but we both knew it had to be something new.

Then, a week before graduation, there was the big fight. Sheryl screeched into the parking lot, slammed the door, pushed her way into the dining room, and laid right into Seth. If Hal had been around, he would have stopped it with a look. But he was nowhere to be seen—he'd left Seth in charge—and so Sheryl was un-opposed, yelling about something small—I think it was prom pictures—and making it really big. With an eye to the customers, Seth told her to quiet down. Big mistake. Now she was raging about how she *would not be quiet* because she knew *what was at stake*. Seth just stood there, helpless. Finally she wore herself out and slammed back to her car. Seth returned to work. I wanted to shoot a look at Bev, but she was out shopping with her mother. I was on my own. I finished my soda and stayed where I was. I looked at Seth until I caught his eye. When everything seemed calm, he came and sat down.

For the first time in my life as a flirt—as something more than just a girl—I found the words. They didn't simply appear. I rea-soned them out. I spoke them. Because they were true, and I didn't need anything more than that. "She doesn't deserve you," I said, and before he could dispute it, I continued. "She takes and takes and takes, but she doesn't take the right things. And she doesn't give the right things back. You're going away now. You don't need her. You probably never needed her. She's going to make it hell for you, but it's over. You know that. Free yourself."

He looked at me like I was some kind of oracle. In the best of all worlds, it would've been a look of love, an understanding that I was the one, I was it. But it wasn't that. Instead it was something almost as sweet—that mix of recognition and appreciation. That gift of worth.

A party of eight came in the door, the bell ringing their arrival. Seth didn't say anything. He just stood up and went to seat them.

He looked back at me once before he got their menus. Taking me in, or at least my words. I almost waved.

I don't know what he said to her. I like to think it was *Even Rebecca, the girl at the pizza place, knows you're not right for me*. Whatever the case, by the time graduation arrived, Seth's parents and Sheryl's parents were talking to one another but Sheryl and Seth weren't. I was lucky—it didn't rain that year, so graduation was on the football field and I got to be there. When Seth's name was called, Bev and I cheered at the top of our lungs. We weren't the only ones, so maybe he heard us and maybe he didn't. What was important was that he could have.

Bev and I ran home and changed. Our parents didn't know *what* to make of the situation, but they went along nonetheless. I was wearing a blue dress from Express, the hem just above my knee, the collar a sailor cut. Bev, after buying many runner-up outfits, ended up wearing her favorite pink sweater set and white pants with new flowered sandals. Seth gave us each a hug when we arrived, then went to talk to his relatives. We were stranded— even the pizzeria seemed unfamiliar, decorated with streamers and banners, serving food that *wasn't all pizza*. We had both chipped in to get Seth a present. When he came back, we asked him to open it. It was an address book for him to take to college. (Bev had wanted to write our addresses in it, but I told her that was way too much.) "Ansel Adams," he said with excitement. "How did you know he's my favorite?" Bev (bless her) said it had been my choice, that I had just known. This got us each another hug, and an introduction to some of Seth's cousins.

Our eighth-grade graduation was the next day. We were going to high school now. But first we were going to camp. I didn't want to go. I wanted to spend the summer sipping Diet Cokes and snatching Seth's free moments like fireflies. I argued with my be-wildered parents. I even risked a tantrum. They would not give. *But you love camp*, they said. Arrangements had been made. Checks had been sent. I'd be leaving next week.

As if this wasn't hard enough, Seth was going to be in college by the time Bev and I got back from our respective camps. He looked sad when he told us this, but it was small consolation. That week was an extreme bittersweet.

The dreaded Wednesday, the day before I left, I spent the morning seeing Bev off to camp. There was a slight delay—the bus had a flat on its way to the parking-lot pickup. Bev leaned over to me and said, "Go. It's okay. Just write and tell me what happens." I hugged her tight and ran the thirty minutes to La Rota, stopping a little short to catch my breath.

Seth was there. I looked at him for a minute in the window, my reflection laid atop his body. I knew I would never forget him; I was recording it all now so I would remember him right. Then I walked in, bell ringing, Seth smiling. "The usual?" he asked, and we both laughed. It was a little before lunchtime—nobody else was around. Hal said hi to me and told Seth he'd cover the other tables. So for the first time, Seth and I sat at the table for a whole half hour, him asking about camp, me asking about his summer and college. He stole a slice from me. I didn't care.

Too quickly, we were done. I knew my parents were waiting. I knew I still had packing to do. But I didn't know how to say good-bye.

We just sat there. Then Seth laughed and said, "Look at us!" He said he was sure we'd meet again. He'd come back home and there I'd be, at table seven (I'd never known it was table seven), and we'd talk just like we'd always talked. I went to pay, but he said it was on the house. Then he said, "One sec" and ran back to the kitchen. When he returned, he was holding a neatly folded napkin. This time he had drawn something for me. It was a drawing of a pizza box. In the center he'd sketched a picture of me. And instead of *You've Tried the Rest, Now Try the Best*, he'd written something else. It said, *You're Not Like the Rest—You're the Best*.

I knew I was going to cry. I thanked him and accepted his hug without once thinking it could be a kiss. He wished me luck at camp. I wished him luck at college. The bell rang again as I left. Our last words were *keep in touch*.

I still have that drawing. Whenever I look at it, it makes me happy. That's the moral of the story. That's it.

LOST SOMETIMES

His name was Dutch. We weren't boyfriends, but we screwed all over the place. I'm serious—you name the place, odds are we screwed there. The gym. Burger King. His grandmother's house. We couldn't stop. We decided to go to the prom together to make a statement, and also to see if we could screw there, too.

There were a couple of other gay kids in our school—it was a big school—but all of the rest of them were, like, *sensitive*. With Dutch, though, everything was exactly what it was. We first hooked up at this Christmas party, senior year. You know, the kind you have with your friends a few days before everyone has to go stick it out with their parents. Anyway, the eggnog was ass-knocking. I kinda knew Dutch, but I had no idea what his story was. Me, I was a big flamer. In middle school, they wanted to cast a girl as Peter Pan but decided to cast me instead. No real mystery there.

So it got to be about three in the morning and Dutch walked over and told me I was a little devil. I told him that he was a little devil, too. And sure enough, that's all it took for us to start making out in Kylie Peterson's little sister's bedroom. I mean, her stuffed animals were on the bed, but we didn't care. I'd kissed guys before, but it had never been so *voracious*. I loved it. We didn't go all the way—we figured there weren't any Trojans hidden in the My Little Ponies, if you know what I mean—but it was clear we were already on the way to all the way.

It was a game. I mean, don't get me wrong—it was serious. But it was also a game. I'd say we screwed on our third date, but we didn't go on *dates*. *Dates* makes it sound like dinner and candle-light were the point. But the point was sex. The usual ways and places first, then getting trickier. We didn't want to get caught, but we wanted to come *this close* to getting caught. We wanted to see how far we could go before we got the shit kicked out of us. Sometimes we'd pass each other in the halls—arranging it so we'd walk by each other between every period, but not saying a word, just giving each other that *I'm going to have you soon* stare. And other times he would grab me right there by my locker and thrust his mouth onto mine, and we'd be tonguing it up for everyone to see. It was so screwed up, because the thing that made us the most powerless also gave us such power. We could make them turn away. We could bother them and challenge them and mess them up. You think people are afraid of two boys in love? To hell with that. What people are *really* afraid of is two boys screwing. And even though we weren't about to drop trou in the halls, we were going to let them know we were doing it whenever we could. We always played it safe, condom-wise. But location-wise? Safety was not the first concern.

The first-floor boys' room. The showers of the locker room when everyone was in class and we were skipping. The couch in the faculty lounge. The boiler room. The second-floor boys' room. The lighting room in the auditorium, against the movie projector. Room 216, second lunch block. The roof of the cafeteria when everyone else was under us, chattering. The art room, with paints. The third-floor girls' room. The 400 aisle of the library.

We were only caught twice. Once I said I was helping to look for his contact lens, which must have fallen on his fly. The other time the art teacher found us. I thought he'd been watching for a while before letting us know he was there, but Dutch said his shock was real. He didn't say a word to us. Just saw what was going on, turned red, and left.

We weren't exactly the popular kids. But we were damn popular with the unpopular kids. The girls especially, this army of goth older sisters—they didn't want to hear about us having sex, but they admired our spirit. We weren't the prom types, but as the time approached, Dutch said to me, "Wouldn't it be cool to screw at the prom?" and I said, "Yeah, I guess it would." I kinda wanted to go anyway, but I wouldn't've told him that. I didn't want him to think I was taking anything too seriously. He'd already told me we were going to split up at the end of the year, because in college there would be new dicks to play with. He said it like he was joking, but you can't tell a joke like that without meaning it at least a little.

We weren't going to spend any money on the prom or anything cheesy like that. No limo, no tuxes, no tickets. We were just going to show up and do it our own way. While other couples were talking about flowers and cummerbunds, Dutch was telling me to not wear button-fly pants, "for easy access." That night while biting his neck, I drew blood.

The prom was at some hotel, which made it very easy to crash. As everyone was pulling up to the front door in their gowns and their stretches, like it was the movie premiere of their new life, Dutch and I were smoking with some busboys by the service entrance. He was flirting, I was nervous, and when the pack was finished, the busboys pointed the way to the ballroom.

After we slipped in, I looked around the room and felt strange. It wasn't that it was beautiful—it was just a hotel ballroom, with round tableclothed tables and white balloons with our class year printed in orange and blue, our school colors. But seeing it made me feel . . . sentimental, I guess. I had been to proms before, but this was the one that was supposed to be mine. This was a memory I was supposed to be having.

As I looked around at my classmates all dressed up, Dutch was scouting out a place to screw. He didn't want to start in the men's room, because that would be too obvious a choice. I insisted that going under one of the tables was a bad idea, since people would be sitting down soon, and then we'd be trapped. We walked back into the reception area. People didn't seem surprised to see us, or to see that we hadn't dressed up. They weren't disappointed in us, because their expectations had never been that high to begin with. It bothered me.

Then Dutch pulled me into the coatroom and made me feel a little better. You know what it's like to look at someone and realize they're hungry for you? The thing I loved the most about Dutch was that he never stopped grinning—even if his mouth was serious, his eyes were in on the joke. He enjoyed me, and that's what kept us going and going and going. He found the most expensive coat in that coatroom, then took a turn into the back, threw the coat on the floor, and led me on top of it. Button-fly access, yeah. Condom, nice to meet you. I could hear everyone outside not hearing us. I could hear the empty hangers ping against one another as my shoulder hit into the racks again and again. Dutch would stop and smile, and I would smile back and keep quieter than usual. I'd feel his breaths catching, measure the distance between them to know he was close.

After we were done, he squeezed me tight for a moment and then said, "All right—back to the prom!" I made the foolish mistake I'd made at least a few dozen times already—I thought, for that one millisecond of hope, that this might be the moment, the occasion that he would say "I love you, Erik." Even if he didn't really mean it. We'd been screwing around for long enough that I knew it was a conscious decision on his part to never use those words with me. And because he held them back, I restrained myself, too. The two times I'd slipped and said them, he'd just smiled and said, "No, you don't."

Dutch was hungry again, this time for food. So we put our clothes all back in place and returned to the ballroom. We found our goth girls and their punk boys, and we ate off their plates, which they let us do because they thought that was punk, too. We were crashing, which was nothing new. But this time I actually felt like I was interrupting, too. When the DJ started spinning hip-hop and pop tunes, Dutch made fun of everyone who went to dance to them. I could tell that some of our friends had intended to dance, but now felt awkward about it. I kinda wanted to dance. The best I could do was lure Dutch away, so the goth girls could get down and the punk boys could shimmy to their punk hearts' content. I put my hand on Dutch's ass and whispered, "We're not done yet."

We walked into the men's room just as half the football team was peeing out the beers they'd tailgated before heading over to the dance. I thought, *We really shouldn't be doing this*. But Dutch's boldness carried me on. He held my hand and opened the stall door as if it was the door to Cinderella's carriage. When he closed it and locked it behind us, I could hear the jeers. One of the guys pounded on the door, and I jumped. Dutch looked ready to start fighting . . . but soon the jeers faded. The football players left. Other people came in, but they had no idea what we were up to—not unless they looked down and saw the two pairs of legs.

This time we didn't go all the way. We just kissed and groped, and it was almost like the beginning. Only it didn't feel like the beginning, because I knew the beginning had passed a long time ago. Dutch was murmuring how hot I was, how great I was, how cool this was. Usually I could lose myself in that for hours. Usually that was how I knew I was okay. That being me, that doing this, was okay. I loved that he said these things, and I loved that when I was with him I could believe they were true. Which is different from loving him. But in some ways more powerful.

There was a spot on his back that caused him to shiver whenever I touched it a certain way. I loved that, too. I loved knowing his body that well. But it only worked when we were lying down, relaxed, quiet. When we were pressing against each other in a bathroom stall, there wasn't that kind of vulnerability, that kind of control. It was like we were now one thing, and everything outside the stall was another. As opposed to when we were truly alone together—then we were each one thing, and the charge came from combining the two.

After a while our mouths and hands took their usual course. When we emerged from the stall, this kid I'd been friends with in seventh grade—Hector—was at the sink, washing his hands. He looked in the mirror and saw us emerge. And then he shook his head, as if to say, *What a waste*. And I thought, *You asshole*. I turned back to Dutch and gave him a long, hard kiss, right in that mirror. Us against the world.

Here's the thing—even if it was just sex, even if he didn't say "I love you," even if I knew it wouldn't last, you have to understand that I would have been alone without him. I would have been so alone.

I held his hand as we went back into the ballroom. I couldn't get him as far as the dance floor, but we found friends to talk to, joke with, tease and be teased by. I could see a few teachers and administrators wanting to say something to us about our clothing choice, but as long as we held hands, it was like we were invincible. When the prom queen and prom king were announced, I half expected it to be us. I was a little disappointed when it wasn't, because I would've liked nothing more than to have walked on stage with Dutch, to give him that royal kiss in front of the whole school, to prove that we'd been here, unafraid.

The DJ announced that there was only one more song until the prom song, and that couples should reunite and head for the dance floor. Dutch looked over at the DJ on the stage, then grinned and sparkled even wider. He held me by the hand and led me in the dance floor's direction. Then, just as we were about to get there, he pulled me to the side, into the shadows. He pointed, and I saw what he'd seen—a small crawl space under the stage, beneath the music. "Come on," he said, hunching down, heading inside. I followed.

It was a maze of dust and wires and reverb. There was barely enough room to sit upright, so Dutch lay down on the floor, staring up as if the bottom of the stage was full of stars. I crawled next to him, and he immediately rolled to his side and kissed me. His hand ran over my back, then down below my waistband.

The first sounds of "In Your Eyes" came through—the drum and the bell, the steady heartbeat. And then Peter Gabriel's first words—*Love, I get so lost sometimes*. I heard them so deeply at that moment. Even though Dutch was pressing into me. Even though I was turned on and warm and with him . . . I thought to myself, *I'm missing something*. I stopped kissing Dutch back, and the minute I stopped kissing him back, he knew it and he stopped kissing me. But he didn't pull away. He didn't let go. Instead he pulled back enough to see me. To read me. And I stared back at him, daring him not to move. I thought it again—*I'm missing something*. A few feet away, couples were dancing to their prom song, holding each other tight. I was missing that. And at the same time, I was here, under the stage, being held in this different way. Looking into his eyes. Having him look into my eyes. Staying quiet. Just watching. Feeling our breath, his hand still on the small of my back, on the skin. I realized I would always be missing something. That no matter what I did, I would always be missing something else. And the only way to live, the only way to be happy, was to make sure the things I didn't miss meant more to me than the things I missed. I had to think about what I wanted, outside the heat of wanting.

I had no idea whether Dutch noticed any of this, or what he was thinking. When the song was over, we made sure we'd been hanging in the moment before a kiss, not in the moment after one. Then we crawled back out from under the stage and walked back to our friends. I forgot to hold his hand.

Later that night when we were naked in my basement, naked afterward, he said it to me. And even though it was too late, I didn't say, "No, you don't." Instead I kissed him once, quickly. Then we lay there, and I let time pass.

PRINCES

The minute I hit high school, the minute the train station was only a walk away, I escaped into the city and danced. I had been practicing since I was seven—practicing to be that kind of body, the kind that gets away. Right after school, two days a week. Then three. Then four. The *Nutcracker* in winter, the big recital right before summer. I outgrew my teacher and his storefront studio. Cut class to audition for a modern dance studio in Manhattan. Treated my acceptance like the keys to the city.

When you're a boy dancer, your progression through the *Nutcracker* is like this: First you're a mouse, then you're a Spaniard, then you're a prince. I could feel my body changing that way, from something cute and playful to something strange and foreign, then something approaching beauty. You start off wanting to be a snowflake, to be a character. But then you realize you can be the movement itself.

I loved watching the boys, and I loved being the boy who was watched. Not as a mouse, not as a Spaniard. But now, as a prince.

I doubt my parents knew what they were getting into when they let me go to that first dance class. I know some fathers justify it by saying it will help when the boy grows up to be a quarterback, when he has to dance past the linebackers. I know some mothers tell other mothers that it's so much better than staying on the couch all day. My parents never really discussed the subject with me. They came to the *Nutcrackers*, they came to the big recitals, and they came to the conclusion that I was gay. Not every boy dancer is gay, or grows up to be gay. But come on. A whole lot of us are.

My brother Jeremy came to most of the performances, too. When he was five and I was ten, he got all worried that our Jewish family was starting to celebrate Christmas, with all of the red, green, and white costuming going on. It was only when he realized he was celebrating me instead of celebrating Santa that he was all for it. Five years younger than me, always a kid in my eyes. Whether he knew I was gay or not didn't really matter to me. He wasn't going to be a part of that part of my life.

That part resided in the city. Specific address: the Broadway studios of the Modern Dance Workshop, housed in a rent-by-the-hour space between Prince and Spring in SoHo, with a view of a publishing company across the street. I had to audition four times in order to get in—there were only twenty students, mostly city, some suburban. Six guys, fourteen girls. The instructors were either older dancers who'd been worn down into being choreographers or aspiring dancers looking for a day job to support their auditioning habits. There was Federica Rich, a middle-aged footnote of the footlights. There was quiet, unassuming Markus Constantine, who looked at us not so much as teenagers but as potential trajectories, mapping the mathematics of our every movement. His counterpoint was Elaine, who'd just graduated from the dance program at Michigan, and clearly belonged to the dance-as-therapy school. She was always examining her reflection in our wall of mirrors.

And Graham. At twenty-two, he was only five years older than me. He hadn't gone to college; he'd danced his way across Europe instead. He was beautiful in the way that a breeze is beautiful—the kind of beauty you feel gratitude for. From the minute I saw him behind the table at my fourth audition, I knew I would be dancing for him. To make him watch, so I could return the watching.

I was not the only one. We'd all tell stories about Graham and treat them like facts, or glean small facts and turn them into stories. Carmela had heard that he'd been an underwear model in Belgium. Tracy said he once dated one of the male leads at Tharp, and that when he'd left, the lead had drunk himself into depression. Eve said this wasn't true; the dancer had been from Cunningham, not Tharp.

I wanted to be the one to find out the truth. I wanted to become a part of the truth, part of the story.

Mostly, I hung out with the girls. They weren't competition. As for the other boys—only one or two were a real threat. Connor had the inside track with the teachers, since he'd been at MDW for two semesters now. Philippe was much stronger than he was graceful, but he was also named Philippe, which I had to imagine gave him an advantage. As for the others—everyone trusted that Thomas had been accepted because of his trust fund; Miles seemed intimidated by the sound of his own footsteps; George leaped like a gazelle but landed like a lumberjack. Modern dance is forgiving of many things, but it still discriminates against the balance-impaired.

From the minute I got on the train, I felt I was already in the city, already a part of that rush. But when I got into the studio, the city ceased to be anything but a traffic buzz in the background. That room contained a world.

On the train ride back, I would try to stay within it. I would re-play Graham's single nod to me a hundred times over, watching it from every angle. If he said anything to me, I would gather the sentences like a shell seeker. Sitting on the orange reversible seats, jutted back and forth by the rhythm of the rails, I would try to re-member all of my movements. Inevitably, the ones that came back to me the most were the errors—the slight wobble of the ankle, the unfortunate and unintended dip of the arms. My memory be-came slave to the corrections I would need to make. More so if Graham had noticed.

I could have called one of my parents to pick me up when I got into the station, but I was never ready to see them, never ready to concede that I was home so soon. So I walked the mile home. My body, having just been sitting for a half hour, reawakened to a new kind of fatigue—not the adrenaline exhaustion of having just fin-ished, but the unoiled hinges of afterward, when everything catches up with you and your body lets you know how it truly feels. Sometimes I loved that ache, because it felt like an accomplish-ment. Other times I was tired of everything.

I always stayed until the last possible moment of class, and then sometimes a few of the girls and I would run to Dojo for a yo-gurt shake or a cheeseburger. By the time I got to my street, subur-bia was empty of cars, of noise, of movement. Even the reading light in Jeremy's room was off, the new chapter dog-eared for the night. My parents' room emanated a blue television glow; if I went close to the window, I could hear the sound of law-and-order sus-pects being caught, or the roll call of the news. By the time I passed their doorway, my parents were usually asleep, even if the television wasn't.

I was seventeen, halfway toward eighteen, and I had learned something nobody had ever taught me: Once you get to a certain age, especially if a driver's license is involved, you can go a whole day—a whole week, even—without ever seeing your family. You can maybe say good morning and maybe say good night, but everything in the middle can be left blank.

I saw Jeremy a few minutes every morning at breakfast. He was starting to really grow, almost thirteen. His awkward voice didn't faze me, but the way his body was beanstalking, beginning to fit into itself, was strange. I knew there were probably things I should be telling him—but then I figured that I'd figured it all out without the help of an older brother. I wanted him to be independent. So I left him alone.

Did I know him at all? Yes. He was class-president material, in a town where that was more a measure of affability than popularity. He would grow up to be the boy every girl's parents wanted her to bring home. He was ingratiating without being grating. He was, I imagined, *an okay guy*.

And did he know me at all? He knew me as the brother who was always leaving. So maybe the answer was yes.

One of the reasons I was so happy to avoid my house was that everyone else was deeply involved in the preparations for Jeremy's Bar Mitzvah. My own Bar Mitzvah had been stressful enough— forget coming of age, it was more like a see-how-many-times-his-voice-can-crack contest. (The answer: roughly 412 times in one morning service.) The experience left me with a sheaf of savings bonds and little else. Jeremy's, if anything, was going to be more elaborate. Jeremy seemed less bothered by this than I was.

He deferred everything but the Torah portion to our parents, and appeared grateful and interested when such things as appetizers and candle color were discussed. After my recommendation for a bacon-flavored cake, I wasn't consulted.

Two more weeks. I only had two more weeks to put up with the preparations. My mother had made me pick out my tie over a month ago. I was all set.

At class, we didn't acknowledge our parents. No, that's not true—we were willing to acknowledge their faults. I kept relatively quiet during these conversations, because I had less than the other kids to check off on the dishonor roll of slights and abuses. Carmela's dad had left and her mom had given up. Eve's stepmother nearly broke Eve's leg. Miles's parents were in a constant state of disowning him. Although he'd never say it, the girls knew he was working two jobs to pay for tuition. Every now and then Thomas, our trust funder, would strip a twenty from his parents' billfold and we would all draw hearts on it before slipping it into Miles's gym bag.

Graham never talked about his parents or where he'd come from. When he said "home," he meant his basement apartment in the East Village. I imagined it so clearly, down to the rag rug on the floor and the incense holder on the bedside table. Sometimes I would play an infinite game of Twenty Questions with him, trying to use each question to narrow him down even further, to get to his one single answer. Did he live alone? Yes, if you didn't count the uninvited mouse. Was he happy in New York? Yes, but in a different way than he'd been happy in Barcelona or Paris. What did he think of *Center Stage*? That God was cruel to make Ethan Stieffel straight.

From the way he criticized my dancing, I knew he thought I

had a chance. You don't need to go to too many classes to know the difference between a teacher who points our your errors because they are beyond help and need to be pointed out as an obligation to dance itself, and the instructors who tear you down because they think you can rebuild in the proper way. Graham didn't hold back his corrections, but he didn't hold back his praise, either.

We each had to perform in a piece, and Graham chose me to be in his. While Elaine dangled her dancers in Debussy, Markus knit together swaths of Schubert, and Federica fastened onto flamenco, Graham decided to make a suite out of recent Blur songs. "An aria of dislocated longing," he called it. "A dance for the anonymously lovelorn," I answered. He nodded, happy with me.

Practice was different now. He would touch me, guide me, manipulate me into the right contours, the shape of his vision. I was used to this, but not in this way. This was not the *Nutcracker*. This was personal. I was prince now of a kingdom that was still being defined.

There was a movement I couldn't get. A turn with arms outstretched. I could not get my arms to match his direction—or maybe it was that he could not get his direction to match with words. My arms spread too much like wings, then too much like broken branches. They embraced too much of the air, then they did not hold the space tight enough. Graham came behind me and mapped my arms with his, held my hands and made every point align, wrist to shoulder. I closed my eyes, taking in the angles, the arcs, his breathing against my neck. When he let go, I stayed in the pose. *David's slingshot*, he called it, and I knew I wouldn't get it wrong again.

When we were done, he asked me to join him for a drink. I

knew it wasn't a date. I knew he wasn't asking me out. But what my mind knew, my hope ignored. It was my hope that was disappointed when I came out of the changing room to find a whole entourage waiting for me. It was my hope that faltered when Carmela said, "Are you coming with us or not?"

But my hope was stubborn. When Graham held back so we'd be side by side on the sidewalk, my hope ignored everything else and held on to the single fact of his proximity, his choice. He led us from the back, calling out directions to George and Carmela until we made it to Beauty Bar, which used to be a beauty parlor but now served cocktails. The decor was still Retro Beautician, with half-dome hair dryers attached to the backs of many of the chairs. There were six of us, and Graham was the only one who was legal. We gave him money and he represented us at the bar, returning with Cosmopolitans stemmed through his fingers, perfectly balanced.

He chose to sit next to me and then he chose to talk to me for the next hour. We talked about Paris, and I tried to erase my family from as much of our family vacation as I could. He touched my arm for emphasis and left it there. Our legs came into perfect contact. He glinted at me.

Is this really happening? I thought. Then I saw Miles on the other side of Graham. Noticing. He smiled at me, as if to say, *Yes, it is happening.*

I didn't feel that many steps younger than him. He wasn't treating me that way. If I didn't feel like his equal, then at least I felt like he was welcoming me into the range.

I wanted every word to last for hours, every gaze to last for days. I wanted to confiscate all our watches, banish all the clocks. But inevitably Graham looked down at his wrist and realized there was somewhere else he needed to be. There was no question, no discussion, that the rest of us would go when he did. Staying would be like trying to act out the trick after the magician had left the stage.

Graham hugged us all good-bye. My hug lasted a little longer, had a little tighter squeeze at the end.

I wanted to kiss him. I wanted him to want to kiss me.

But not on the street corner, not with George and Miles and Carmela and Eve there. We all dispersed, me and Miles walking together to the subway. I was practically floating—and then I realized that Miles, in his quiet way, was floating, too.

"Wasn't that amazing?" he asked. "I mean, that place. And that drink. And everything. I can't wait for life to be like that, can you?"

No, I told him. I couldn't wait.

I wasn't planning on waiting.

When it was time for us to part, he opened his arms for an embrace. I figured this was now the way we would all say good-bye.

As he hugged me, Miles said, "You're pretty cool, you know."

"You're drunk," I told him.

He pulled back with a smile and said, "In a way." Then he said good night again and disappeared with a wave.

On the train ride home, I wondered if I should have asked for Graham's phone number, what it would be like to hear his voice at midnight, the last sound before going to sleep. It was late when I got home, but not too late. Still, my father was waiting for me when I came into the kitchen. He did not look happy.

"Where have you been?" he asked.

"A few of us went out after. For dinner."

"Was it better than the dinner you were supposed to be home for?"

And it wasn't until then that I remembered—a Family Dinner. I had promised, and I had forgotten.

"Your mother is very upset," my father added.

"Well, I'm sorry."

"You don't sound very sorry."

There was no winning. None whatsoever.

"I'm going to bed," I told him.

"You will be home for dinner tomorrow. Do you understand?"

"It's not that difficult a concept."

"What did you say?"

"I said fine. *Fine.*"

The next day at class, Federica had us doing exercises most of the time, so I didn't get a chance to have Graham Time by myself. I did notice him watching me, though. Singling me out. At one point I winked at him and he laughed.

I was home in time for dinner, but not in time to set the table. Jeremy had done it dutifully in my place.

As soon as the food was served, conversation turned immediately to the Bar Mitzvah. Reply cards were in, and with less than two weeks to go until the big day, it looked like there were more attendees than my parents had been planning on.

"All your cousins are bringing their boyfriends," my mother said with a sigh. "I knew we shouldn't have let them bring a guest. All it takes is one of the girls to bring a boyfriend, and suddenly they all have boyfriends to bring. We haven't even met these boys. Except for that Evan, and he was *not* family material."

I don't know what started me thinking. Maybe it was the

fact that two of my cousins were exactly my age. Maybe it was the notion of *family material*. But suddenly I had something to say.

"I didn't know Diane and Liz were allowed to bring guests," I said.

"Yes, *and* Debbie and Elena. You knew that."

I put down my fork. "So I assume this means that I can bring a guest, too."

Now my father put down *his* fork. "What do you mean?" he asked, with a tone of genuine mystification.

"I mean, I can bring someone. Right?"

"But these are the girls' boyfriends," my mother said.

"What about *my* boyfriend?" I found myself asking.

Pure silence at the table, loud shouting in each of our heads. Except Jeremy's. He just watched, transfixed.

"What boyfriend?" my mother asked.

"He doesn't have a boyfriend," my father answered. "He's just being stubborn."

"His name is Graham," I said. "He's in my dance class."

It was the name that did it. The name that made it real. For all of us.

"Jesus Christ," my father said, pushing his plate away.

"There are already too many people," my mother added quickly, somewhere between diplomatic and petrified. "There isn't enough room."

"There is for Diane and Liz and Debbie and Elena's boyfriends."

"But that's different."

"How is that different?"

"It just is."

"That's bullshit."

Now my father looked truly pissed. My mother was still trying to salvage her argument. "We don't even know this boy," she said, having already forgotten his name. "It's not like you've brought him home for us to meet."

That was brilliant. "Why in God's name would I want to do *that*?" I was shouting now, near tears. Trying desperately to keep those tears in, so my parents wouldn't see them.

"Honey . . . ," my mother soothed. But it was too late for her to make it better.

"Don't leave this table," my father said, anticipating my next move.

So I left. Threw my napkin on my plate, went to my room, closed the door.

How many times had we acted this out before?

Usually I slammed the door. Locked it.

I was beyond that now. I didn't want them to hear a thing.

Like I was already gone.

If I'd had a car, I would have driven all night. But instead I let my mind do the driving. It took me to Graham's apartment. Into his arms.

My mother knocked and told me there was still food in the kitchen.

I didn't answer.

My father walked by. I could hear his footsteps slow for a second, then move on.

When Jeremy came by, his knock was quiet, as if he thought I was already asleep. Because I felt bad he had to see everything, I told him to come in.

He stayed in the doorway. Was it because he didn't want to disturb me? Or was he afraid I'd shout at him, too?

I didn't know.

I was about to apologize for dinner, to let him know it really didn't have anything to do with his Bar Mitzvah. But he surprised me by speaking first.

"Do you love him?" he asked.

"Who?"

"Graham."

He was serious. I could see it on his face. He was trying to process it all, and he was serious.

"Yes," I said. "I probably do."

He nodded, and I knew there was something else that I should say. But once again, I didn't know what those words were. I wasn't used to being a brother.

And that nod. Was he accepting me? Or was it about something else? He looked determined. But I had no idea why.

"Good night," he said, closing the door.

I had planned on sneaking away in the morning, avoiding them all. But when I got to the kitchen, Jeremy was already there, our parents in orbit around him, trying to get their things ready for work. Neither my mother nor my father said anything about the previous night. Neither acknowledged that this was anything but an ordinary day. But Jeremy . . . well, Jeremy did.

He didn't even look up from his Frosted Flakes.

"You're going to let Jon bring Graham to the Bar Mitzvah, right?" he said between spoonfuls.

My parents shot each other a glance. Then my father said plainly, "No, we're not."

Jeremy, still looking at his cereal: "Why not?"

"It's not appropriate. If this were a few months ago, maybe. If this was a longtime thing, perhaps. But not now."

"How do you know how long it's been?" I asked.

But my father didn't rise to the question. He just said, "End of discussion."

Now Jeremy raised his eyes from his breakfast and looked straight at our mother.

"I want to invite Graham," he said.

"That's sweet," she replied. "But really, it's too late."

Jeremy went on. "If you don't want to invite him as Jon's date, he could come as one of my friends. I know Herschel can't make it, so Graham can come instead."

Instead of answering my brother, my father went after me. "What have you been saying to him?" he asked. Then, turning to Jeremy, "What did he say to you?"

"He didn't say anything to me," Jeremy answered. "I just think if Jon wants to bring his boyfriend, he should."

"The answer," my father insisted, "is no."

He gathered up his briefcase, as if this truly was the end of discussion. My mother and I stood still, waiting—for what, we didn't know. I watched Jeremy. He looked pained. I wanted to tell him to stop, it was okay. But I stayed silent and he did not. He looked right at my father this time.

"If Jon can't invite Graham," he said slowly, surely, "then I am not having a Bar Mitzvah."

"What?" my father asked, as if he hadn't heard right.

"You don't have to do this," I said.

"No," Jeremy told me. "I do."

Why? I had done nothing to deserve this. Nothing.

"We'll talk about this tonight," my father said before storming out. He didn't even kiss my mother good-bye, like he always did.

My mother looked at me and said, "You see what you've done?"

I couldn't take it. I know I should have stayed by Jeremy's side. I should have talked to him. Maybe talked him out of it. But it was too much. I did the only thing I knew how to do—I left. I gave Jeremy a squeeze on the shoulder before I did. That's what I could give him. And I gave my mother a kiss, probably because my father hadn't. Then I was out of there. Free, but not.

I was in a daze through school and the trip into the city, but seeing Graham brought me to all of my senses. At first I wanted to tell him everything. Then I just wanted to tell him something. And eventually I would have been satisfied with telling him anything. We worked pretty much the whole day together, the same Blur songs playing over and over as he led me through the steps, as I showed him what I could do. His sweat on mine, his hand guiding my body. I felt such sureness there. Nobody could tell me what I was doing was wrong.

Thomas invited some of us to stay at his house overnight. His parents were away and he wanted to have a party. We didn't trust Thomas to catch us from our leaps, to make the right entrance at the right time. But we *did* trust his parents to have a large, unlocked liquor cabinet and plenty of space to crash.

It was Friday. There was no reason for me to go home, and plenty of reasons for me to stay.

I called the house and Jeremy picked up.

"Tell Mom and Dad I'm staying over at my friend Thomas's," I told him. I even gave him the number.

He took it down, repeated it to me. We hung on the line for a second.

"Hey, Jon?"

"Yeah?"

"Are you really going to Thomas's?"

"Yeah."

"Not Graham's?"

I heard a little hope in his voice. "Nah," I said, "but I'm hoping he'll be there. Thanks again, by the way, for this morning. You really don't have to do that."

"No, I want to," he assured me. "It's important."

I was trying to think of something to say to that, but Jeremy quickly told me our mother had gotten home, so he had to go.

I told Thomas I was in the clear, then I went to find Graham. He'd just changed from the shower, his hair dripping perfectly.

"A bunch of us are going to Thomas's," I said, all casual. "You wanna come?"

I thought for a moment he was going to say yes, his smile was such a welcome one. But then he shook his head and said he had other plans. *A date?* I wondered immediately.

"A friend's birthday party," he said, as if reading my fears.

So a bunch of us went up to Thomas's—Miles and I were the only sleepover guests; the rest were all city kids. Thomas's place was nearly palatial, an Upper East Side mansion-apartment. We had the run of the land. Soon we were drinking, flipping cable channels, and gossiping about all the people who weren't there. For one night—this big city night—I was an adult and I was treated like an adult. Like my opinion mattered. Like I had things to say. Like I could do what I wanted because I could judge my own consequences. We started talking about families and I bragged to everyone about what my brother had done, made it sound like we'd both stood up to our parents. Of course, I didn't tell them who I'd named as my boyfriend, or even that I'd given him a name. I made it an argument over principle—an argument I'd won.

"So what's going on with you and Graham?" Miles asked later on, when we took over the bunk beds in the guest room. Everyone else had left by now, except for Eve, who was making out with Thomas. A kind of host gift. I thought Miles was a little bit drunk and I wasn't sure whether or not I was, too. I knew Graham would tell me, if only he were here.

"I don't know what's going on with me and Graham," I said—and Miles laughed. "What?" I asked.

"Nothing," he said. And then his voice changed to another voice, a gentler voice, as he wished me good night.

The next morning—more like afternoon, really—we woke up before Thomas. Miles cleaned the living room a little while I took a shower. Then another hour passed and Thomas still hadn't emerged from his room. There was no way we were going to interrupt his closed door, so the two of us decided it was safe to leave. I asked Miles what he wanted to do.

"Why don't we check out where Graham lives, see if he's around?" he replied.

"But we don't know where he lives!" I protested.

"Ooh, look," he said, picking up the phone, "I got some magic in my fingers. I just press four-one-one, and . . ."—he gave Graham's name and the East Village and asked for the address—"presto!"

There were messages on my cell phone from my home number, but I didn't check them. My parents' voices didn't belong anywhere near this world. As Miles and I rode the 6 train downtown, we tried to piece together all the events of the previous night. Miles seemed disappointed in Thomas, and I wondered if he had a crush on him. (I hadn't known Thomas was into girls, but I hadn't really cared, either.)

I didn't think we actually were going to show up at Graham's doorstep. But when we got there—he lived next to a pizza place on East Ninth—Miles started to head straight for the bell.

"What are you doing?" I asked, not without some alarm.

"Don't you want to see if he's in?" he replied. I couldn't tell if he was taunting me or just trying to help.

"I'd rather just bump into him," I said.

So we got a pizza, then wandered around the block a half dozen times, until a lady on the stoop next to his asked us what the hell we were doing.

Neither Miles nor I wanted to go home, so we dragged our wandering farther, checking out the tattoo parlors on St. Mark's and getting an overpriced latte to share at the Starbucks on Astor Place. Finally we found ourselves back at the dance studio—we were allowed to use it on weekends for rehearsal. It was better than going home.

And there he was. We walked into the studio and Graham was the only one there. Dancing each part of his piece, rehearsing for all of us at once. I felt such intimacy toward him then. An intimacy that was stolen, yes. Like staring at someone dreaming.

I watched him, and I could feel Miles watching me watch him. I didn't try to hide it.

It was only when the dance was through, when the soundtrack had moved on to the next song, that Graham looked over and we made our presence known. Applauding, Miles and I walked into the room. Graham seemed surprised to see us, but not unhappy.

"So you survived your momentary brush with the lifestyles of the rich and infamous?" he asked. We told him a little about the party. He didn't talk about *his* party, but he did say that his friends hadn't made it to a midnight showing of a movie he wanted to see.

"We should go," I said.

"Cool." Graham looked at me. "You free now?"

"Yeah," I said, trying not to sound too eager.

"Miles?"

And Miles did the most amazing thing. He said, "No. I gotta get home. You two'll have to make do without me."

Part of me was afraid Graham would use this as an excuse to back out. He said he was sorry Miles had to go. And he asked me if I could wait ten minutes while he showered and changed.

I said it wouldn't be a problem.

"Thank you," I said to Miles as soon as Graham had hit the changing rooms.

He shook his head. "I don't know which of us is the bigger fool."

I asked him if he was really going home and he just shrugged and said, "We'll see. I gave away my shift, but maybe I can get it back."

Graham came out of the changing room with his shirt unbuttoned one step lower than most guys would have dared. I was wearing a black stretch T made for a dancer's figure. We were quite a pair, entirely in place on the SoHo streets. On the ten-minute walk to the theater, we talked mostly about the dance and how it was coming along. When we got to the box office, he insisted on buying my ticket. I got us sodas.

The movie didn't matter. As far as I was concerned, it existed to give us its glow in the darkness, to give us faint voices to hear at a distance from our thoughts. I wished I had gotten us only one soda. I moved mine so the center armrest would be free and clear. The theater was almost empty, the movie at the end of its run. I tried to focus on the scenery on the screen—the English manor house, the droll goings-on. But it was Graham, Graham, Graham. Right beside me. Only a gesture away.

His arm was on the armrest. I moved mine closer. Then closer still, so our sleeves were touching. He was looking at the movie, but he was feeling me closer. And closer. I turned to him. He turned to me. I moved my hand on his. I traced my fingers around his fingers, then ran them down his sleeve, down his arm.

He pulled away.

I wasn't ready for his movement. The choreography suddenly confused me. This was the wrong improvisation. He pretended to be moving for his soda. When he put it down, he kept his arm in his lap and his eyes on the screen.

Two more hours. The movie lasted two more hours.

When it was over and the credits were rolling, he leaned over and asked me what I thought, if I was ready to go. *Ready* was the last thing I felt, but *go* was pretty much at the top of the list.

He wasn't going to say anything. For a second I wondered if my mind was playing tricks, if what had happened hadn't really happened after all. But once we were in the lobby, once we were in everyday light again, I could see the awkwardness of his stance, his expression.

When you dance, you measure distance as if it's a solid thing; you make precise judgments every time two bodies exist in relation to each other. So I knew right away the definition of the space between us.

We moved to the street, the rest of the audience dispersing in animated clusters around us. It was still daylight, but it was almost dark.

"Jon," he said. Just the way he said my name. Every part of me but my hope gave up right then.

"But why?" I asked.

He put his hand on my shoulder, and even now I loved that.

"I really think you're fantastic," he told me. "But I think you might have the wrong idea."

Later on, I would want elaboration—every possible kind of

elaboration. But right then, I only wanted to leave. He asked me if I was okay. He asked me if I wanted to get coffee, or talk some more. He was kind, and that made it better and made it a whole lot worse. I had to go.

I walked around the city a little, but even that was too much. I took the train home, defeated. The only saving grace was that my parents were already out when I got home.

Jeremy was there, though, babysitting himself, which wasn't something I'd been allowed to do. He was watching a movie on cable, studying his Torah portion during the commercials.

"Hey," he called out when he heard me come in. "How was it?"

At first I didn't know what he meant—how was what? The movie? The date? The ride home?

Then I realized he meant the sleepover at Thomas's. Which he thought I'd spent with Graham.

"It was okay," I said, throwing my bag down on the floor and sitting next to him on the couch. He muted the TV.

"Did you have fun? Did you tell Graham about the Bar Mitzvah?"

"Look," I said, "I don't think that's going to happen."

"No, it is!" Jeremy said, looking totally energized. "Mom and Dad gave in. I knew they would."

I couldn't believe what I was hearing.

"How?" I asked.

"I just told them I wouldn't do it," he said. "And they knew I wouldn't."

"Are you kidding?"

He looked at me, confused. "No. Not at all. It seemed stupid to have a Bar Mitzvah if I wasn't going to stand up for something that's right, you know."

I knew he was trying to help. I knew he was trying to take my side. But still I couldn't help but see him as my younger, inexperienced brother who didn't know anything about anything.

"Do you understand what you're doing?" I said, my voice rising. I wanted to shake him. "Don't think I don't appreciate it. But are you crazy? Think about it for a second. Not about Mom or Dad. Or me. Think about you. This is a very big deal, Jeremy. All our family. All your friends. Do you really want all your friends to see your brother and his *boyfriend*? There has to be a line somewhere, doesn't there? Do we get to sit together? What do I introduce him as? Do we get to dance together? What do you think everyone will say, Jeremy? Your Bar Mitzvah will go down in history as The One With The Gay Brother And His Boyfriend. You can't want that. You *can't*."

But even as I was saying it, I was looking at his expression and I was thinking, *Yes, he does. He is ready for all of that.*

I didn't know where he got it from. Not my father or mother. Or me.

"Jon," he said, "it's okay. Really, it's okay."

This twelve-year-old. This stranger. This brother. This person sitting on the couch with me.

It was too much. I had to leave again. Only this time I wished I had the ability to stay. I wished I could stay there and believe him.

But it was too much. It was all too much.

I tried to sleep through Sunday. My mother came into my room and asked me to try on my suit one more time.

"I have to hand it to your brother," she said. "He makes one hell of an argument. Especially when he's right. Sometimes I guess you need to be bullied by the truth. I was caught up in everything else." Then she smiled at me and apologized for how stressful the past few weeks had been. "I just want to live through it," she said, straightening my tie. "I want it to be a perfect day. Although at this point, I'd settle for really good."

She asked me if I'd asked Graham. I said yes.

She asked me if he was coming.

I said yes.

It's not that I wasn't thinking—I was thinking way too much. I was thinking of what Jeremy was willing to do, and how I'd be letting him down if I didn't deliver on the situation I'd thrown him into.

"Does he know to wear a suit?" my mother asked.

Again, yes.

She put her hand to my cheek and said, "I look forward to meeting him."

I knew that took a lot.

I thanked her.

My father let his lack of complaint speak for him.

The whole day I wanted to pull Jeremy aside and tell him: *You're believing in love more than I do; you're standing up for someone who is less than deserving.*

I was trying to keep my mind from Graham, from Monday afternoon when we'd see each other again, but that was an impossible thing to do. Every hour that passed was loaded with thousands of thoughts—and no conclusions.

Somehow I made it through school. Somehow I made it into the city. Somehow I walked through the door to class without trembling.

He was waiting for me, waiting with Eve and Miles to rehearse the third movement of the Blur piece.

"Hi," he said, a little hesitant. Then, after he sent Eve and Miles to rehearse in a corner together, "How are you?"

"Been better," I said. "I'm really sorry—"

"No, *I'm* sorry. I didn't mean to give you the wrong idea. And at the same time, I don't want you to think I don't care about you. I do."

"I know," I said. Maybe I did, maybe I didn't. Maybe he did, maybe he didn't.

We hovered around our apologies, our acceptances.

"It's okay," I said, finally. "Really, it's okay."

Maybe I even believed that. But my body didn't. It had lost the thread of the dance, grasping instead at ulterior intangibles. My arms opened too wide, then held too fast. My turns ended in the wrong place.

Graham did not say a word. Not until Eve and Miles were involved. Then he tried to minimize the damage I was doing, the errors of my way.

I could sense Miles watching me, wondering what had gone wrong. But Graham was always within hearing distance. It wasn't until after the dismal rehearsal that Miles could come over, put his hand on my shoulder, and ask me, *"What happened?"*

He took me to a used bookstore café around the corner. He bought me tea. He sat me down. He didn't ask what happened again, because it was so obvious. The language of my posture translated to defeat.

"Jon," he said. Quietly, gently, the word pillowing out to me.

And I told him. What had happened, what hadn't happened. Even more than I'd realized before. Eventually I found I was talking more about Jeremy than I was about Graham. About how I had set up this picture in my brother's head of what my life was like, and how he had fought for that picture. That had made it more real. And I still couldn't deal with it. I was still running away instead of fighting, too.

"Your brother's pretty brave," he said. "I can't imagine . . ."

I waited for him to finish the sentence. What couldn't he imagine? Doing it himself, or having someone do it for him? I waited, but he left it open, closed.

I looked at him, studied the thoughts right underneath his expression. Most dancers find their confidence in dancing. Right is mere millimeters away from wrong. Failure is always louder than success. But there is an accumulation of all the things you don't do wrong, and that becomes your confidence. You can even get to the point where that confidence lasts longer than the dance. Seconds at first. Then minutes. Then maybe it'll be there when you're walking into a party, or meeting people after a show. You know you have something desirable, and you know you can move. But for Miles, the confidence wasn't there. Instead, there was something even more marvelous—the trying.

Suddenly, it occurred to me. I was looking at Miles twisting the coffee stirrer around his paper cup. I was thinking of him, of me, of Jeremy.

"You could be my boyfriend," I told him.

"I could?" The coffee stirrer fell to the table, still looped.

"For the Bar Mitzvah. You could be my boyfriend. Would you?"

"Be your boyfriend?"

"For the Bar Mitzvah."

Miles looked at me strangely. "That's one hell of a proposal," he said.

"C'mon . . . it'll be fun."

"Now, you *know* that's a lie."

"Are you free?"

"Are you crazy?"

"Please," I said.

"You want me to *pose* as your boyfriend—the boyfriend you've never had—in order to make sure your brother—God bless him—didn't take a stand for nothing."

"Pretty please," I said.

"You're so stupid. You know I'm going to do it."

For the first time that awful day, I felt something approximating happiness. "I will owe you," I told Miles. "Anything your big heart desires."

"Anything?"

He seemed happy despite himself.

And so it came to pass that on the morning of my brother's Bar Mitzvah, I was introducing Miles to my parents as Graham, but telling them to call him Miles, since that was what all his friends did.

He looked amazing, in a blue suit, white shirt, and purple tie. He'd taken a train, a bus, a subway, and a cab to get to the synagogue, and he'd made it exactly on time. My parents, overwhelmed by all the greetings coming their way, were polite without really registering. Jeremy pulled away from the rabbi to shake Miles's hand, to tell him he was glad he'd come. He turned to me and said Miles was exactly what he'd pictured. I didn't know what to say.

Miles was going to sit in the back, but I wanted him beside me. So we sat in the front row. When his *keepa* kept falling off his head, I reached up and pulled out one of the bobby pins keeping my *keepa* in place. Instead of handing it over, I leaned into him and touched his hair, securing the *keepa*. Maybe nobody was looking, but it felt like everyone was. I didn't turn to see what was true. I just looked at him and his nervous smile.

The service began, and all focus turned to Jeremy. It was so strange to sit there and watch him for two hours. I don't think I'd ever considered him—really *watched* him—before. It wasn't that I hadn't realized he was growing up—I was always waiting for the next stage, the first hint of body hair, the voice's awkward, jagged plunge. But I was always mapping him out against my own progression—as if he was somehow having the same life just because he had all the same teachers. Now I wasn't seeing him in terms of age, or in terms of me. I was just seeing him. Five years behind me, but somehow with his shit together. He'd tied his tie himself and it was perfectly knotted. He chanted over the Torah portion as if it was something he was born to do. And he made eye contact. I swear, as he spoke it was like he looked each of us in the eye. Bringing us together.

I should have felt proud, but instead I felt awful. That I had let him down so many times, that I had been a horrible brother. That he loved me anyway. That maybe he knew more about life than I did, even if I'd had more experience. Because knowing about life is really about knowing how it should be, not just how it is.

It hadn't occurred to me that this would be Miles's first Bar Mitzvah; it hadn't occurred to me that he might be more nervous than I was. During the rabbi's sermon, his leg started to shake. I rested my hand on it for a second, giving him as much of my calm as I could. He accepted it without a word. I used the open prayer book as a phrase book to tell him things, pointing to words, rearranging the scripture to spell out our own verse. GOOD. IS. PLENTIFUL. YOU. ARE. ALL. WISDOM. SHINING ON A HILL.

When the service was over, when we were all getting up to shuffle to the reception, he straightened my tie and moved some of the hair from my eyes. My mirror. I fixed the back of his collar. His mirror.

Jeremy had sneaked into the reception hall before the service, banishing one of our cousins to a kids' table so Miles could sit with our family. I wondered what we all looked like to Miles, as we said our prayers and lit our candles and danced a whirlwind *hora*. I tried to put myself in his place, and realized we looked exactly like what we were: a family. These strangely tied together individuals trying desperately to keep both ourselves and one another happy. Succeeding, and failing, and succeeding. When Jeremy called me up to light one of the thirteen candles on the cake, he said the kindest things, and I knew he meant each and every one. He talked about me teaching him how to ride a bike, how to swim, how to kick an arcade game in just the right place to get a free play. He was remembering the best of me. The way he spoke, I almost recognized who he was talking about.

I stayed up for the final candle, for my parents at their proudest. The love I felt for them then—I knew I meant that, too. It wasn't something I had to think about. It was there, unexpectedly deep. I hadn't been running away from that, or even from them. I had been so focused on my destination that I'd forgotten all the rest.

At the table, my mother asked Miles how long he'd been dancing. They talked *Nutcrackers* while my father watched, taking it in. After the *hora*, the dancing grew more scattered, the sincere thirteen-year-old girls and the jesting thirteen-year-old boys doing their sways and muddles as my older aunts and uncles kicked up (or off) their heels and used the same moves they'd learned for their weddings decades ago.

Miles and I watched from the sidelines, and I gave him the

anecdotal tour of my family's cast of characters. At one point Jeremy came over and asked, "So, are you guys going to dance or what?" But I wasn't sure Miles wanted to, so I put it off. Miles was doing me enough of a favor. Dragging him onto such a dance floor would be cruel.

I tried to imagine Graham there in his place, but I couldn't. It was laughable. Impossible. Stupid.

Finally, after two or three songs of sitting in the folded-chair gallery, picking at the mixed salad with blueberry balsamic vinaigrette, Miles turned to me and said mischievously, "So . . . are we going to dance or what?"

"Yes," I said. "Let's."

Miles smiled. "It's about time."

Just because two people can dance well on a stage to prearranged choreography doesn't guarantee that they will be good partners in a simple slow dance. When Miles took my hand in his, there was no guarantee that our arms would fit right. When he put his other arm around my back, there was no guarantee that it would feel anything but awkward, unrehearsed. When his feet started to move, there was no guarantee that my steps would match his.

But they did.

As if we had rehearsed. As if our bodies were meant to be this. As if we were meant to be this. Together.

He closed his eyes. He was with me, he was elsewhere, he was with me. I looked over his shoulder. My mother smiled at me and I nearly cried. My aunt and uncle smiled. Jeremy watched, as a girl tugged on his sleeve, telling him to hurry.

I closed my eyes, too.

The sound of a dance. This dance. The ballad of family

conversations, clinking glasses, plates being cleared. One heart-beat. Two heartbeats. The song you hear, and all the things beside it that you dance to.

When it was over, Miles pressed my back lightly and I squeezed his hand. Then we separated for a fast song. Instead of jumping off the dance floor, we jumped into the fray. We joined Jeremy and his friends, the aunts and the uncles. We electric slid. We celebrated good times (come on). We cried *Mony, Mony*. As a crowd, part of the crowd, together.

It was fun.

When the next slow song came on, there was no question. I reached for him, and he let me.

"May I?" I asked.

"Certainly," he replied.

But just as we were about to start, there was a tap on my shoulder. I looked to my side and saw it was Jeremy.

"May I have this dance?" he asked.

I let go of Miles and turned fully to my brother, raising my hand to his.

"Uh . . . sure," I said.

Jeremy looked at me as if I were an idiot. "Not with you," he said. "With *Miles*."

My brother wanted to dance with my not-quite-but-maybe-so boyfriend. I could imagine all his friends watching—his *eighth-grade* friends watching. Talking. Our family. Our parents.

"Why?" I asked.

He winked at me. I swear to God, he winked at me. And then he said, "I want to make Tom *insanely* jealous."

"Let's go, then," Miles said, laughing. And with that, they left me. Stunned. They took the dance floor, laughing and awkward and wonderful. I felt such love for both of them. Such love.

I looked over to Jeremy's friends, who were all watching. I wondered which of the boys was Tom. If Jeremy was serious. Then I looked over at my father, at everyone else who was watching, confused and excited. *Something was happening.* I knew my father would blame me. I knew he would say all of this was my fault. And I would take it. I couldn't take any of the credit for my astonishing brother, but I would happily take all of the blame. If it could be in some way my fault, then I would know I'd done something right.

I would stay to find out. And stay, and stay, and stay.

It is never, I hope, too late to be a good brother.

BREAKING AND ENTERING

People never change the place they hide their keys.

It was right after midnight. Back when it was summer, back when I had some reason to hope. Cody's parents were out of town for the weekend and Cody's keys were locked in his car, seven blocks away. He took me around back and we walked quietly through the night foliage, listening like thieves for the neighbors who would notice, the ones who might tell. I wasn't supposed to be there, wasn't supposed to be the boy Cody loved, wasn't supposed to see when he moved the flower pot and revealed the spare key underneath. He didn't say anything, didn't swear me to secrecy. He just held his breath a little as he squeezed past me to the door, ran inside so the alarm wouldn't sound. When I walked in, I had to call out for him. He reached me before I got to the light switch. We found ourselves in the dark.

Now it's afternoon, four months later. Cody is gone, but the key is still in its hiding place. I don't know what I'm doing here, only that I have to be here, doing this. Breaking and entering. The breaking has already happened, is always happening. So I reach for the key. I fit it into the lock. I enter.

I should be in school. I should be enjoying the first breaths of the last gasp of my senior year. I should be living my days like they are the best days.

Cody is in a place I've never been, with people I've never met. Somehow I allowed him to step into the future without me.

From a schedule I saw back when all such things were hypothetical, I know he is sitting in an English class right now. I can picture him there. I can see him slumped back and doodling. I can see him after class, walking over the green. Or asleep in his dorm room, eyelids closed. The pattern of his breathing. I can see it clearly, and none of it is true. It is only my version, which is imagination.

This place is real. These steps are real. I am in his house, surrounded by the house silence that is not like breathing at all. There is only background. It is a sound like loneliness—enough to let you know you're there, but not enough to fill you with life.

I have very few memories of the kitchen, but it's still hard to be in here. It's wrong and it's stupid and it's hard. I can't deny what I'm doing anymore, not with the sink dripping and cereal bowls in the sink. I remember the sliver of the kitchen I saw that night when the refrigerator light knifed it open to us. Four in the morning, he could stand there naked and not be afraid. I wore his robe and took comfort in the thought that I was making it a little bit mine. Everything we did that night seemed so brave and so doomed. Brave because we felt doomed, doomed because we felt we'd always need to be brave. Even getting orange juice at four in the morning. Looking into that light.

I want him to know I'm here now.

I want him.

The sink drips and drips and drips. Cars pass outside. The key is still in my hand, fitting.

There are things he told me. His fear of stormy nights. The time he kissed a boy in summer camp, pretending it was a game. His father's affair. The strength of his love for me, even if he didn't always call it love.

I remember these things. They are my proof that we actually happened. He wouldn't have told me these things if I hadn't meant something to him. I have to hold on to all the truths he gave me. Even when they seem so incomplete.

I drive past this house all the time. I've made it on my way to school. Sometimes I slow down. I don't know why. Only that it's where he once was, back when we were.

We'd said we'd keep in touch. But touch is not something you can do from a distance. Touch is not something you can keep; as soon as it's gone, it's gone. We should have said we'd keep in words, because they are all we can string between us—words on a telephone line, words appearing on a screen. But they cause more complications than clarity. On the phone, there are always voices in his background. On the screen, there are always the sentences saying he has to go.

I know he is gone, but this house is not. That's the best way I can explain it. I cannot touch him, cannot press my hand against his body, cannot feel the warmth spread from his skin. The best I can do is touch the things he has touched the most. I just want a moment in his bed. To trace.

The stairway is lined with photographs. He is every year old. That night, the one that's slowly becoming a lifetime ago, he walked me through all the class pictures, all the bad haircuts and awkward smiles. Him as a seven-year-old ring bearer and him as a fourteen-year-old on the lip of the Grand Canyon. That night, he held up a flashlight and he told me about the photographs like they were words in a long sentence. Then he turned the flashlight off. He took my hand and led me forward.

His room looks the same. His parents always leave the light on. To ward off burglars. To pretend someone is home. I don't have to touch the switch. I don't have to do anything but walk inside. I know he took things with him. I was there when the car left. I stood there camouflaged by his other friends in a group good-bye. I saw the milk crates of books and the sheets and the toiletries crammed into the backseat and the twine-tied trunk. But the room doesn't seem to have suffered from the subtraction. Most of the books remain on the shelves; I see a copy of *Demian* and wonder if it's the one I gave him or the one he already had. I take some solace that there aren't two, that a book he would associate with me has made it to his room at college. I cling to the associations.

The bed is made, ready for his return. I put my face to the pillowcase, hoping it might smell like his echo. Instead it smells like laundry. I take off my shoes. I curl up on top of the sheets. I clutch.

We fought over who it would be easier for. He said I was lucky to be in the same place, to have such a familiar world around me, to have the friends here and the knowledge of where I was. I said he was lucky to be getting a new beginning, to be moving on.

I don't know what I thought I'd find by breaking in here. An envelope with my name on it, awaiting my arrival? Cody himself, standing in front of the closet, deciding what to wear? An entirely empty room, as robbed of his presence as I am? No, not really. Maybe all I wanted was what I find now: rest. Simple, uncomplicated rest.

The light fades. The day ends. The door opens, and I'm asleep.

It isn't until she's in the room that I stir. I sense her presence before I can register it. She stands there for a beat before saying anything.

"Peter?"

I open my eyes. There is light, there is color, and there is Mrs. Baxter standing in the doorway, looking like she's come home to find all the furniture rearranged.

I am surprised she knows my name. I've met her probably a dozen times, but it was always in passing. I was a sound in another room, a door about to close, a phone call answered before she got to it. I'd never felt like a boy with a name to her. Cody had wanted to keep me separate.

"Hi, Mrs. Baxter," I say, sitting up and turning out of bed. Staring at my shoes unlaced on the floor.

"Is Cody here?" she asks. But she's looked around. She knows the answer.

"I don't think so," I tell her. If I bend over to put on my shoes, I will have to turn my head entirely away from her. That seems rude, so I just sit there.

I always thought Cody looked more like his father—the same shoulders, the same dark hair. But there's something in Mrs. Baxter's eyes that looks familiar. I don't know whether it's their shape or color or just the way she's looking at me now, trying to piece the situation into sense. I get that glint of Cody from her.

"How did you get in?"—this is said calmly, almost kindly. She's not alarmed. I don't get that from her.

"I used the key." I've let go of it, lost it in the folds of the blanket. I reach over for it now, hold it in my palm for a moment before offering it back to her.

She doesn't take it. She has her own keys in her hand.

Unjangling car keys and house keys and probably office keys. Her hair is shorter than I remember. When Cody left, she must have cut her hair.

I reach for my shoes and then stop. I feel the key in my hand and I stop. I don't look right at her and I don't look all the way away from her. She is standing next to Cody's desk and I am looking at the photos on the bulletin board. I am looking for me. I am looking for some sign of me.

If we were strangers, she would be calling the police. If I had been a part of her life, if she had known me, we would be talking. But instead we're somewhere between strangers and familiar. So the questions fill the room in their silence.

He pulled away from her. He never told me that, maybe didn't even know it. But all the times Cody talked about his father and everything his father did wrong, he never said anything about his mother. Not to me.

I know the situation is my fault, so maybe that's why I finally say, "You're probably wondering why I'm here."

And she doesn't say anything. For just a moment, she gives me a look that makes me think that, yes, it's possible she *does* know exactly why I'm here, more than I know myself.

"I'm so sorry," I continue. And it's like the last word is a hurdle and I can't leap it, because something in the word snags my voice and suddenly I am giving everything up. I am letting my shoulders fall and I am feeling myself become the absence, feeling myself become that gasp and sob.

I could never say what I was to him. He never let me know, because maybe he was afraid that if I knew, everyone else would know, too.

But keeping my guard up has taken too much. Now I just want

it to end. I've always wanted the happy ending, but now I'll just settle for the ending.

Here. In his room. How had we managed to erase the rest of the world? Because that is what it took for us to crawl into the naked silence, into the truth of the thing, into the doomed and the brave.

Now the light is on and his mother is here and I am on the edge of his bed and my head is in my hands. My eyes are open and I'm not seeing a thing because I am so lost inside.

I hear the hit of the keys as she puts them down on the desk. I see her legs as she walks over. I feel the weight of her as she sits on the bed next to me, not touching.

"Peter?" she says gently.

And I say it again. "I'm sorry." And again.

He is so far away and he doesn't feel it like I do. He doesn't feel it.

We sit there. Breathing, thinking.

"You don't have to be sorry," she says. "I'm just a little confused."

I can tell from the sound of her voice that she's not looking at me, just as I'm not looking at her. We're both looking in front of us now. At the empty doorway.

"You miss him," she says. And my first instinct is to deny it. Deny us. Deny her. Deny myself. To admit one thing is to admit everything. It has always been that way.

So instead I wonder what my silence says. Because even if I cannot say *yes*, cannot say *so much*, I also can't bring my voice to say *no*, to say *I don't really miss him at all*.

Quietly, so quietly, she says, "I know."

I turn to her then. And her eyes are closed. Her coat is still on.

Her left hand is gripping her right hand. Then she opens her eyes, sees me, and smiles. Not a big smile, or even a welcoming one. But a small, rueful smile. It could be kindred, or it could just be sad.

"It's not easy," she says, in that voice that mothers have, that mix of unwanted knowledge and small consolation. "Whatever you had—I don't know exactly what it was, and that's fine. But it must not be easy for you. You miss him, and that's okay. But you have to figure that if it's too hard to hang on, then maybe you should let go."

I want to ask if he's mentioned me.

"What is his room like?" I ask instead. "Up there."

She looks at me for a moment, deciding something, then says, "It's fairly small. Not much bigger than this room, but for two people. His bedspread is blue. It matches the carpet, which is something we couldn't have known. We got him a refrigerator. One of the small ones. His roommate seemed very nice. I think they get along."

"Does he call?"

She nods. "Yes. We talk for a few minutes. Every few days."

If I had been the same age. If I had gone to the same school. If I was in that room right now. There's no way to know if we would have lasted. There's no way to be sure, and plenty of reasons to doubt it. I just wish I'd had the chance. That is one of the things I miss the most—the chance to make it work.

The whole time I thought that I was figuring him out, wearing down his hesitations. But really I was wearing myself down in order to spend that one last hour, that one last sentence.

"Peter," Mrs. Baxter says. And it's almost the way he says it. That mix of love and reproach. "You can't do this. Look at me." I do, and it's not his eyes I see. No, it's something completely separate. A different kind of concern. "Do you understand? You can't do this."

I start to say I'm sorry again. For using the key. For being here, when all she probably wanted to do tonight was take off her coat, sort through the mail, wait for the call.

"It doesn't work," she continues, unclasping her hands, smoothing her skirt. "What you're feeling right now doesn't work. You can't wander around and think the wandering will call them back. Believe me. I know you don't want to hear the long view, but let me tell you. You are so young. I know it's none of my business. But still."

She sounds surprised by her own urgency, by the fact that she is talking to me this way. I doubt she gets to give advice often. Certainly Cody never took it, to the point that he never mentioned her giving it.

She stands then. Puts her hand on my shoulder and lifts herself off the bed. Walks to the doorway, then turns back around.

"You can stay as long as you need to," she says, "but don't do this again. This is the last time."

I know I didn't come here to say good-bye. But suddenly it feels like it is.

She picks up her keys off of his desk and looks at me, at the room, one long time before she steps into the hall. I hear her bedroom door close behind her. Cody's door remains open.

I don't need any souvenirs. I'm sure there are things that I could take that he would never know were missing. But I already have an unlabeled collection of things that are ours. We would ink our skin blue and sign messages with our thumbprints. We bought our favorite movies for each other. We made our own yearbooks to sign for each other, a month or two before he left.

The yearbook I made could be with him now, or maybe just hidden somewhere in this room. I say good-bye to knowing the answer. I say good-bye to the sheets that don't smell like him. I say good-bye to the robe that's forgotten what I felt like. I say good-bye to the part of myself that misses him so much. I say good-bye to hope, but I also say good-bye to hope's disappointment.

I turn the light off as I leave. Then I remember, and turn it back on. Leave the room as I found it, but not untouched.

I call out good-bye to his mother. She calls good-bye in return.

I head back down the stairs. I head through the kitchen. I open the back door, then close it behind me. It is only then that I realize I still have the key. I go to the flower pot, which I hadn't moved back in place. It is dark now outside, but I can still see the outline of where the pot should be sitting, the faint impression left by the key. I return the key to its hiding place, then conceal it once more.

People say good-bye, and then they take one last look. I am a few steps away when I turn to his window. And there, as I watch, the light goes out. The door closes, and I walk away.

SKIPPING THE PROM

Our story was going to be that we'd overslept, but in the end we told the real story, which was better. Not more exciting or daring. Just better.

From the beginning, Kelly didn't want to go to the prom, and neither did I. I think I would've gone if she'd wanted to, and vice versa. But we wanted to spend the night with each other instead.

We'd been going out for five months, and we knew we wouldn't be going out in another five months. It was a conversation we had by never having it; in the same way we'd be graduating from school in June, we knew we'd be graduating from home in August, and that meant graduating from our relationship as well. We were sad about this, but not sad enough to change it. We wanted to be realistic. We prided ourselves on our realism.

It was hot that night, so I was wearing a T-shirt and an old pair of shorts, and she was wearing some sleeveless Gap top and cutoffs. We'd discussed getting dressed up like everyone else, but decided to go for comfort instead. Instead of heading someplace fancy, we went to our local diner. It was amazing to see it so empty, and to know that we weren't going to bump into anybody from our grade. Even though we were a couple, it was rare for us to get a chance to go out on our own. We had a group we called "the group" because it wasn't defined enough to have a more elaborate name. It was just this mass of friends we moved with from time to time—in school, then from school, then after school, and (maybe once a year) instead of school.

Now it was just us, so we spent most of dinner talking about everyone else. Because that, in essence, was what we had in common: our friends, our classes. And also the confusions we tried to hide, the pressures we tried to resist. We loved the same movies— dark, twisted comedies with semi-sentimental endings. We each read the newspaper in the morning. We wanted our emotions to read like poetry, even if the poetry we wrote never managed to read like poetry, because we never really figured out how to put the emotions there.

She wasn't pretty, but there were moments when I found her beautiful. I was just starting to figure these things out. I liked her breasts, I liked her smile . . . and I loved her eyes. They had at least five colors in them, but I could never tell exactly which ones. As we gossiped over grilled cheese, I rubbed my bare ankle against hers. Not to be provocative or possessive. Just because it felt good to have that spot on me touch that spot on her.

We ate fast, like we always did. It was still light out at eight, so we drove over to my mom's house and hung out there for a little. I don't think my mom even knew it was prom night; she was simply home on a Saturday night like she always was, with her son and her temporarily adopted daughter swinging by to keep her company for the space of a TV show. By the time the credits were rolling, dusk had settled outside the window, and we were ready to go.

We had spent the last week planning this, not telling anyone for fear that they'd want to join us. With the group, any set of plans was also an invitation.

Now the rest of the group was safe in a Sheraton, wondering where we were, but not for too long. As we drove through the newly settling night, Kelly and I pieced together what we knew about what they were wearing, who they were sitting with. We placed bets on who would be the king and queen. We cast our own votes.

We got to the soccer field about ten minutes later. It was behind our old middle school, with a parking area all to itself, sheltered from view. I parked the car, turned off the headlights, and the two of us took the bags out of the backseat. These were the true fruits of our planning—our way of imprinting ourselves onto the evening, without having to wear a gown or a tuxedo.

We walked up to one of the goals—metal-framed and orange-netted. Kelly took out a string of paper lanterns from one of the bags. Neither of us was tall enough to hang them on the goalpost, so I had to lift her onto my shoulders. Then I lit candles and handed them up to her, trying to cup the flames as I did. When we were done, it looked like something strung out from a haphazard luau. But we loved it because it was peculiar. It wasn't what we thought it would be, but we were used to that.

There was a streetlamp perched over the field, even though there was no street in sight. By its light, we unpacked the rest of the bags—blankets, cheese and bread, more candles, music player and speakers, chocolate. We were intellectual virgins, so instead of bringing contraceptives, we brought books of Margaret Atwood's poetry and Sylvia Plath's prose. And at first we read to each other, by that mix of candle and streetlamp—not just from the books, but from notebooks and Xeroxes, our own observations matched with the observations we wanted to make our own.

Then we lay back, rolling up unneeded sweaters under our heads, leaning into each other for light touches and deeper holding. We talked about everything that was about to happen—graduation, the summer, college—without talking about what would happen to us. We kissed, groped. The night stayed warm. Then we stared up at the sky, searching for the stars that weren't quite there. We started to narrate a prom of our own making, taking it for granted that we were both picturing the same things as we said them.

"Right now, Alison Shaw is slapping Aiden across the face with her bouquet, because Samantha finally told Alison about her and Aiden hooking up."

"Poor Cynthia is sitting at the table, afraid to dance."

"Brett has to be drunk by now, so he's singing along loudly to the wrong song."

"Jeanette and Jeremy are dancing together, and they don't realize anyone else is in the room."

"Whoa—I think Brett just puked."

"But Jeanette and Jeremy didn't even notice."

Then we went quiet, slowing the world down to the pace of our breathing. We fell into a trance of almost-sleep, shifting softly, touching in murmurs. We, too, could feel like we were the only ones. We lost track of time because we felt like time had lost track of us. Months from now, our relationship wouldn't break up so much as dissolve. But here was the opposite kind of dissolution—

that evaporation into a common moment, far from nothing and also far from anything else.

It was Kelly who looked at her watch, who realized it was almost midnight, the end of the prom. She jostled me up, and I reached past the still-wrapped food for the music. I pressed play . . . and nothing happened. Kelly took the player from me and looked at the blank screen.

"You have a charger in your car?" she asked.

And I said, "No . . . but I have a car."

The candles in the paper lanterns had long since burned out, so now they hung like grown-up balloons from the goalpost. I watched them stir as I walked past. Turning the car on, I woke up the radio and cranked the volume as loud as it could go without waking the neighborhood. Then I left the door wide open, the inside of the car dimly gathering light from its small plastic chandelier. By the time I got back to Kelly, a song was just starting.

"Well done," she said.

We held each other as the song started to play. I don't want to say what song it was; that, more than anything, remains ours. It's not really a song you can dance to—it's a song meant for holding on. The temptation might have been to hold tightly, to pull each other so close that there was no distance, nothing between us. But instead we held lightly, so we could see each other, so we could look at each other's faces and live in each other's thoughts as well as our own. In my car, radio waves were being translated into sound, carrying across air, translating back into this loose communion, this song shared.

Did I love her then? Yes, in a genuine way. But I knew it wasn't everlasting, and that was okay. We had the time that we had, and we would be together for the rest of it.

I think I want to leave us there. I want to leave us in that corner of the middle-school soccer field, lit by a streetless streetlamp, listening to our prom song pour out from an old Buick. Let's stay on this song, before it turns to something else, before it switches to a commercial. Let me hold on to this the way it was, before I knew anything else.

A ROMANTIC INCLINATION

Their eyes met across the room, at an approximate inclination of twenty degrees.

Sallie gazed at James.

James gazed at Sallie.

And at once, both were illuminated.

Through the convex lenses of his glasses, James stared at the beautiful mass of matter named Sallie Brown. She seemed larger than life (a magnification of forty-nine times, to be precise). There she was, thoughts diffusing into her notebook, paying attention to the lecture that he could not bear.

Her magnetism was something he could not resist. He just kept exerting energy in her direction, stealing a glance once every 6.6 seconds. His heart grew in volume and defied gravity at the very sight of her, with her vibrant sense of humor and radiant personality providing other coefficients of attraction.

Sometimes, her smile would raise his body temperature two Celsius degrees.

James Helprin was very much in love, for that millisecond.

And so, to add symmetry to our story, was Sallie Brown. Her attraction toward James was not just one of surface value—she liked his inside parameters as much as his outside exponents. The thought of him with her made her head spin like an unbalanced torque and made her heart slide like a kilogram weight on a frictionless pulley.

Sallie Brown desired a romance of great intensity, one that would relieve her from the pressures of her daily life. She needed a buffer from collisions, a balance when her equilibrium was threatened.

And so, periodically, she looked over at James, with James returning the glance with an equal and opposite magnitude at different periods.

Yet Sallie and James had both life and the laws of physics working against them. You see, Sallie Brown and James Helprin were good friends.

Which adds a certain friction to our equation.

The minute their eyes truly met, that fateful day in AP Physics class, both objects were unprepared for the introspection that followed.

Sallie, no stranger to loving, laughing, and losing, was immediately shocked by how serious she was about James. He had long been a constant to her, one that she often relied upon when there were too many unknowns in her life. Did she really want to send their friendship to infinity by liking him?

The crests of every relationship, Sallie figured, were always followed by troughs (and crests again, if you had the patience—which she didn't). She imagined their attraction turning to repulsion, just like that between a pith ball and a like-charged rod.

My God, she thought. *Would I polarize him?*

She thought of all the work that it would take to maintain equilibrium. She had only so much potential energy to give.

Would it be enough?

Meanwhile, James was having thoughts parallel to Sallie's. The look in her eyes had given him a shock. He started to wonder if their "going out" would reduce to zero everything they had. Friendship had long been the basic element of their relationship. Now, both of them contemplated change. Yes, as Lenz had observed, change can turn on the source that created it, creating a force opposite to the best intentions.

James knew that the road to a simple harmonic relationship would be a hard one to follow. The critical point could only be reached through the passing of three states, each one causing a change in speed and the refraction toward or away from the norm.

And James seriously doubted that he and Sallie had the chemistry—or, in this case, physics—to make it.

If it is to be assumed that Newton was correct (as is the general consensus), to every action there is always opposed an equal action. That is to say that love always goes against a certain gradient. Sometimes risk. Sometimes popular opinion. In this case, regret.

Yes, James feared that liking Sallie would lead him to regret. He would regret liking her in the first place. He would regret breaking off their friendship. He would regret it when, after the statistically assured breakup, they would avoid each other like oil and water.

James did not want Sallie's and his friendship to consist of meetings between classes and periodic waves in the halls. He knew that if their lives had to revolve around each other, they'd grow bored (not to mention dizzy). The damage would be done—the recoil irreparable.

After the initial impulse, James wondered, *would the momentum remain constant?*

Sallie's doubts were only reinforced by her textbook. It defined a "couple" as "two forces on a body of equal magnitude and opposite direction, having lines of action that are parallel but do not coincide."

Would we ever intersect? she asked herself.

She feared fusion would only bring fission, with the mass deficits too great and the energy spent too consuming to make the romantic endeavor worthwhile.

James, having a larger surface and cross-sectional area than Sallie, was worried about the strain that would possibly put a damper on their combined molecular activity. He calculated that as the length of their involvement grew, so would the tensile strain.

He also feared the work that would be needed when he and Sallie wouldn't be together. Using $W = Fd$ as his guideline, James figured out the work that it would take to keep their relationship at a constant force when he and Sallie were more than a mile apart. Furthermore, if he wanted to reduce the force (and, therefore, the work), he would have to slow down love's acceleration by massive proportions.

With a girl like Sallie, a constant velocity with little to no acceleration would not be acceptable (or so James thought).

And yet a velocity increase would require an energy increase. Energy that James would find hard to muster up in this, his hardest year in high school.

Even simple harmonic motion, that romantic-sounding phenomenon, said that acceleration was proportional to negative displacement, which was not an encouraging thought.

Would we lapse into inertia without constant acceleration, requiring a larger force? James asked himself.

Even batteries would be sources of potential difference, thought Sallie.

I don't even know if she's a conductor or an insulator of emotion, James realized.

Boyle's law soon served as Sallie's guide.

According to Boyle, if the velocity of their affair decreased, the pressure would increase proportionally. Sallie was not prepared for this. Her heart had only a certain capacity for crisis.

Finishing her calculations, Sallie finally computed that the stress and strain of a romantic bond with James would be merely a waste of power, damaging the caring she had for him in the past.

She did not want the universe's ever-growing entropy to interfere with her love life.

And thus, James drifted out of the focus of Sallie Brown's affections.

And, in an action so simultaneous that many scientific minds would have been baffled, James Helprin took Sallie out of his romantic-life equation. He knew the friction of a merging of their hearts wouldn't be beneficial. It would be theoretically and realistically wrong.

The next time they found themselves looking at each other, James and Sallie both smiled.

In the end, friendship was proven to be the dominant force. The head and the heart were found to be the joint sources of true romance.

It has been demonstrated.

WHAT A SONG CAN DO

If I didn't have music, I don't know
if I could ever be truly happy.
Happiness is music to me. Like when
I am in Caleb's room, playing
my guitar for him, watching him
close his eyes to listen and knowing
he understands what I am
singing. That is all I need
to make a room full of happiness—
two boys, one love, and a song.

I think the reason my parents wanted me
to play classical music was because
it didn't have any words. They would keep me
as a sound, not a voice. But I had
other ideas. I blew off the recorder,

did not bow to the violin, benched the piano, saved
up for a guitar. Then I used it to write
love songs for boys, and sad songs for love.
I sang myself to find myself
in a language far from my parents'
expectations. I taught myself the strings,
the chords, the fretting. But I did not
have to teach myself the words.
They'd always been there, notes to myself,
waiting for the music to bring them out.

All I had to do was recognize the possible
music and the songs were everywhere.
It is not something I have control over,
no more than I can control the sights
that appear before my eyes. I will be staring off
in class, barely hearing the echo of
my teacher's words, when suddenly
a verse will arrive free-form in my thoughts.

> when I look out a window
> I wish for you on the other side
> even if you're not there
> I can see you in the clouds

As I transcribe the words in my notebook,
I can hear the sound of it in my head.
Many teachers have caught me strumming
an imaginary guitar, trying to find the chords
before they vanish with the next thought.

· · ·

The first time I went out with Caleb,
this happened to me. We were talking
in the park, having a conversation that lasted
the afternoon and the evening,
finding all of our common coincidences,
baring some of our unfortunate quirks.
At one point he went to get us sodas,
leaving me with my thoughts and the trees.
I was elated to have found someone
who could be both interested and interesting.
My thoughts revealed themselves
in the terms of a song.

> *you could be*
> > *the leaf that never falls from the tree*
>
> *you could be*
> > *the sun that never leaves the sky*
>
> *this might be*
> > *the happy ending without the ending*
>
> *this might be*
> > *a reason to try*

When he returned to me, he had two bottles
in his hands, and I was making furious leaps
into my notebook, playing the ghost guitar
and singing solos to the birds around me.
I apologized, embarrassed to be caught
showing myself so early, but he said
it was charming, then asked me if I needed time

to finish my refrain. Perhaps it was because he said
something so perfect, or perhaps it was because
the song made me brave, but I asked him
if he wanted to hear it, and when he said yes,
I sang to him, accompanied only by
the guitar in my head and the beat
of my heart. When I was done, there was
a moment of absolute silence, and I felt
like the ground had been pulled out from under me
and I was about to fall far. But then the ground
came back, as he told me it was wonderful,
as he asked me to sing it to him again.

It is a sad fact of our present times
that it's nearly impossible to turn on the radio
and hear a gay boy with a guitar.
Where are the indigo boys, to show me the way?
Caleb teases me, because while
he has a gay music collection—pop queens
and piano boys—I am, he insists, a closet
lesbian. So I play him some Dylan, some Joni,
some Nick Drake, and I tell him there is
room for me to sing about the two of us
tangled up in blue under a pink pink pink
pink moon. Music, like love,
cannot be defined, except
in the broadest of senses.

My father complains, my mother stays silent.
My father says it's not the music he minds,
but that I play it so loud. They want me

to sing in the basement, but I can't think
with the laundry and the cobwebs—
down there, all my songs begin to have
pipes. So I become a bedroom Cinderella
on a tighter deadline, allowed to sing loud
until the hour-hand tips the ten. Then I strum
softly, sing in a whisper.

I think they would like the songs better
if I left out the names, or changed
the pronouns.

> *No more danger.*
> *Time's a stranger.*
> *When I'm in his arms.*
> *In his arms.*

> *He could break me.*
> *But instead he wakes me.*
> *When I'm in his arms.*
> *In his arms.*

I am not the first person
to avoid the second person.
But I am certainly the first person
to do it in my house.

I never thought I would end up with
someone who wasn't possessed
by music in the same way I am.
I imagined a relationship of duets,

of you play me yours and I'll
play you mine. Caleb doesn't
even listen to the music I like. He dances
instead, frees himself that way
while I prefer the quieter corners,
the blank pages. Part of my music
is being alone, having that time
to shut down all the other noises
to hear the tune underneath.
Sometimes I retreat when he
wants me most. Sometimes
he wants me most when I
retreat. I will let the phone ring,
let the IM blink, and he will know
that I am there, not realizing I am
also in another place. I still sing him
songs before I am ready, sing him
back the moments he has missed.
as if to say, *this is where I was
when you couldn't find me.*
The sound of my voice means
I have returned to him, ready
for a different kind of duet,
that delicate, serendipitous pairing
of listened and sung. He accepts that,
and wants more.

> *black ink*
> *falls on the blue lines*
> *spelling out silences*
> *harboring words*

you think
my love's not the true kind
unanswering questions
do not disturb

but I'm not leaving you
when I leave you
I'm not forgetting
that we're getting somewhere
I'm just trying
to figure my part of this
my place in the world
with you standing there

with you standing there . . .

Our local coffee hangout decides to throw
a weekly open mic night. I decide to go
as a member of the audience, unsure
about playing in a town that knows me
unwell. A local band snarls through
three songs, then a girl from my school
recites poems from a long black book.
I realize I can do this, that I want to be heard,
that it's possible I have something to say.
Word spreads, and all the next week,
my friends tell me to do it, convince me
they'll be there next time. And that is perhaps
the most surprising thing, to feel such support
for this secretive calling. So I sign my name

to the roster, and Caleb makes fliers
on his computer. He slips them into lockers
and strangers from school tell me they'll be there.
Sometimes I've skipped study hall and
practiced in the abandoned stairwell by
the auditorium. Now I'm seeing how many
people have overheard. They have listened in.

I practice past my curfew, past midnight,
into dreamtime. In a moment of weakness,
to fend them off from laying down the law, I tell
my parents I have a gig coming up, as if
they would be proud of me singing in public.
My mother, polite, says it sounds nice.
My father tells me it had better not interfere
with my homework. I tell him it won't,
in a voice that's so ready to leave.
Doors do not slam, but they do not stay open
as I sneak music into the house, as I whisper
my longings to the furniture, my fears
to the ceiling, my hopes to the line of
hallway light that goes off beneath my door.

> *silent night*
> *stay with me*
> *hold me tight*
> *then set me free*
>
> *daylight will*
> *blind me still*

the child's dream
not what it seemed

we search for safer passage
we pray our eyes adjust
we cling to all that's offered
we do what we must

storm outside
thunder warns
deepest fears
since we were born

take me now
show me how
to fight the dark
to find a spark

you are my spark

Who is the *you*? Sometimes when I'm writing
I don't know. I am singing out to the stranger
of my songs.

On Friday, Caleb won't take no for an answer.
We are going out to the club he loves, the one
I've always managed to avoid. He wants to dance,
and he wants me to dance with him. I can't
say no. Even though I dread it, even though
it's not my thing, I will do it for him, because

he has done so much for me. He asks me what
I'm going to wear, and I tell him I was planning
on wearing what I wore to school. He laughs
and tells me to go home and put on something
a little more clubby. For him, this means tighter.
For me, this means darker jeans. When I go home
to change, I don't pick up my guitar, because
I know if I do, I might never leave it.

It's under-18 night at the Continental,
which means there's no drinking,
except for the few hours beforehand.
I carry a small notebook in my back pocket,
although I can't see the music coming to me
here. It is too loud. A singer-songwriter
nightmare. Speakers blasting the *thump-thunk-thump*
of a dance floor mainstay, while the singer belts
the same three lines over and over and over again.
I love this song! Caleb cries, pulling me into
the flashing lights. He looks hot, and everyone else
seems to be noticing. I am lost. It feels like the music
is being imposed on me. I struggle to sway while
Caleb soars. This is his place. This is the liberation
he's found. And there is something beautiful about it,
this closed room where boys slide up to boys
and they find a rhythm that defies everything outside.
The music elevates them, takes their cares away
and gives them only one care in return—this movement,
this heat, these lights that turn them into a neon crowd
feverish in their release, comfortable in their bodies

as they leave them in the synthesized rush.
I observe this without feeling a part of it.
Caleb holds me and pulls me into him and I feel
nothing but the ways my body can't move,
the songs inside that are being drowned out
in this rush. Caleb asks *what's wrong* and I say
nothing and keep trying until Caleb senses it again,
says *what's wrong* and this time I know what's
implied—that the something that's wrong
is me. I tell him I need some water, and when I go
he does not follow.

I get some water and stand on the sidelines.
I watch him and don't recognize him
as the boy I have felt love for. He is joyous
in his movements, holding and groping and swaying
in time with his new partner. And I know it's not
that he likes this other boy, I know it's just part of
the dance, but suddenly I am seeing all the things
I will never be able to give him. I am seeing
that I cannot be a part of the music that sets him
free. And it's seeing it in those terms that does it,
that makes me fill with loneliness. I will stand here
for the rest of the night, and he will dance there.
He has listened to me for hour upon hour, and so
I have dressed the part, I have made the appearance,
I have tried the groove. But in the end he will say
I closed my ears to him, and he will not be wrong.
I take out my notebook, take out my pen,
but the lines remain empty. I cannot think,
I am thinking so much.

. . .

For the first time ever, we drive home in silence.
He is sweaty, ragged, angry, beautiful.
I reach out my hand to say I'm sorry.
He takes it, but gives nothing else away.

That night I go to the basement and play loud
enough to wake the neighbors, but not loud enough
to wake myself. I once read some guy who said
we listen to songs to figure them out, to unravel
the mystery of the words and the tune. I am writing
in order to unravel myself, to find out what
exactly I'm doing, and why.

> *the windows are closed*
> *but the family's still inside*
> *lighting candles in the blackout*
> *walking by the glow*

I'm singing to myself. I'm singing to him.

> *I am standing on the street*
> *the lamplights are a darkness*
> *I've lost my sense of direction*
> *I have nowhere to go*

> *what do I know?*

The next day I return to my bedroom, leaving
only for food, and barely any of that. I sing

the whole day away, playing the guitar
when my voice leaves me, using my desk
as a drum when my fingers start to hurt
from the strings.

> *the windows are closed*
> *but I can feel you on the other side*
> *from the dark of my bedroom*
> *you're just out of reach*

At midnight I hear someone outside my door,
hovering. I yell GO AWAY in an ugly voice.
The someone goes away without a word,
but the hallway light stays on.

> *I am pressing on the walls*
> *no stars around to guide me*
> *I've lost my sense of direction*
> *falling into the breach*

> *what do I know?*

He doesn't call. I know
he is waiting for me to call.
But I don't, and I don't
even know why.

On Sunday my mother finally finds
the courage to stick her head in.
She asks me if everything is okay,
and I laugh.

. . .

Monday is the night I am supposed to play at
the open mic. I'm ready to abandon it, but
people keep stopping me in the halls, telling me
they'll be there. I shouldn't have come
to school. I see Caleb before history and can tell
he's upset, or maybe angry, or maybe both.
He asks me what's going on, and again I use
the least appropriate word, which is
nothing. He asks me if I'm ready
for tonight, and if I still need a ride, and I say no,
and yes. We don't know what to do
with each other, except make plans.

I stay late in the abandoned stairs
by the auditorium, practicing. I'll have
three songs to make an impression,
so I play at least a dozen trying to figure out
which three. As I sing, I realize
how much I miss him. As if the boy
who wrote the words is reaching
across time to point me back
in the right direction. He's saying
*either you were wrong when you wrote this, or
you are wrong now.* I close my eyes, I sing
a song that was not for a stranger

> *When I'm in his arms.*
> *I feel that I could fit*
> *in this world*

for now.
I feel that I could love
this world
for now.

No other places.
As life embraces.
When I'm in his arms.
In his arms.

and I see him.

There's no song that says what I have to
say to him, but it feels like a song,
in that it is something I must express—
there are words inside of me that I must
release. He picks me up at the school,
his radio blaring, and when I turn it down
he shoots me a look. And I tell him I missed
him. I tell him I missed him when he was
on the dance floor, and in our silence
ever since. I tell him our music doesn't
have to be the same, and he tells me
he already knew this, but wasn't sure
if I ever could. He says he doesn't know
if he could ever make me as happy
as finding the right word, the right bridge,
the perfect refrain. And I tell him that music
cannot be separated from life, that you
can't have one without the other, that
he is my love song as much

as anyone can be. But I am still not sure
that I can be his dance. He parks the car and
kisses me softly and says *this is the dance*
and I kiss him hard and say *this is the song*.
Because all of the chords are in a crescendo
and he is their source.

When I show up at the coffee place I see
my friends have arrived on time, which is
nothing short of a miracle. It makes me feel
like I belong to something, that somehow
I have drawn these people together to hear me,
because I know they wouldn't be here together
without me. That means so much.
I am the second act on the list, so while
the first singer torches some standards, I make
a quick dive to the restroom. When I emerge,
Caleb is waiting for me. I can see he's nervous
on my behalf, which makes me want to kiss him
again (so I do). He looks surprised, and
before I can ask why, he tells me my mother
is here. And sure enough, I look over his shoulder
and there she is. Without missing a beat, she
waves. I am now nervous on my own
behalf. I ask Caleb what she's doing here,
and he says *I think she's come to see her son sing*.

I hear my name over the low-grade speakers
that have been set up. I hear the cappuccino machine
burping behind the counter, the sound of mugs
settling on formica, the murmur of strangers.

I stand up on the makeshift stage, really just
an area where the tables have been cleared away.
When I look to my side I can see Caleb
standing right there. And when I look to
the makeshift audience, I see my mother there,
a table to herself, nervous, too, and proud.

I tune for a moment and realize the song
I need most is the one I've just finished,
the one I played all weekend.

> *the windows are closed*
> *but the family's still inside*
> *lighting candles in the blackout*
> *walking by the glow*
>
> *I am standing on the street*
> *the lamplights are a darkness*
> *I've lost my sense of direction*
> *I have nowhere to go*
>
> *what do I know?*

As I sing to Caleb, I know that this song is
no longer about us. Or if it's about us,
it's not about now. I turn to my mother
as I hit the refrain

> *when you hear me,*
> *listen to what I'm saying*

> *when you see me,*
> > *look me in the eye*
> *when you know me,*
> > *try not be frightened*
> *when you speak to me,*
> > *tell me everything*
> > *is going to be fine*

and the most astonishing thing happens, which at first
I can't believe—my mother, in her own quiet way,
is singing along.

Her mouth is moving with mine, she knows
all the words. I am almost thrown from
the second verse, because I am realizing how
deaf I have been. I have misinterpreted the
footsteps in the hallways. I have not seen or
listened or known. And I am near tears, looking
at Caleb, looking at my mother, because for a boy
who has been spending all his time on music,
it's not until now that I know what a song can do.
The second refrain switches a little, but my mother
knows that. We are looking at each other right in the eye
and we are singing to the end

> *when you know me,*
> > *try not be frightened*
> *when you see me,*
> > *look me in the eye*
> *when you hear me,*

listen to what I'm saying
when you speak to me,
tell me everything
is going to be fine

it's going to be fine

the windows are closed
so we stumble to the doors
follow the sound of my voice
saying everything
is going to be fine

At first I don't understand the applause, because
that's not where I am. I am making a new song
out of my mother's expression, the devotion
I've been too caught up to notice, and Caleb's music,
the dancing that we'll do.

This is what a song can do. Our moments are
music, and sometimes—just sometimes—
we can catch them and put them
into some lasting form. If I didn't
have music, I don't know if
I could ever be truly happy,
and if I didn't have these moments,
I would never find music. It is everywhere,
in the air between us, waiting
to be sung.

WITHOUT SAYING

You are in her room, on her bed, as she paces angrily and tells you about Ridiculous Boyfriend #9 and their relationship, which (mercifully) has just ended. She is walking around the room as if she's still in a race with him. She is telling you the story even though you've been hearing it all along.

In a few minutes, she'll fall into the bed and laugh to the ceiling. She'll wish you next to her, and you'll comply. You'll agree with her when she says that guys suck. She'll say you don't count. She'll say you're not like that.

You're only half listening to her. Half listening and three-quarters watching. Ridiculous Boyfriend #9 was a snob, a jerk, too rich, too shallow, too straight, not enough of a pagan. Haven't you said this all before? Hasn't she?

You never say "I told you so," because she knows that you did, and you know that she did it anyway.

"Arrrgh!" she yells in a mock fit of frustration. She's the only person you know who says "arrrgh!" (Charlie Brown doesn't count.) You calm her down. You offer her chocolate.

Does it go without saying that you love her?

Yes, of course it goes without saying.

Milo does not notice Ramona at first. She's like the rest of Michelle's friends. None of them can believe that Michelle is having a Sweet Sixteen. Milo was invited because they needed more boys. But he seems more interested in the centerpieces than in the girls.

Ramona sees him staring at the tulips. He senses he's being watched and blushes.

"Didn't mean to interrupt," she says.

"Tulips," he says. "In January."

She doesn't know what to say to that. Her eyes move to the dance floor, where Michelle is making out with Alex Park.

"She'll end the night pregnant," Ramona observes.

"Good thing I got her a stroller for a present," Milo says.

She doesn't even look at him.

"That's an expensive gift," she says.

"Only the best for my little girl."

They both look back to Michelle, whose bra strap is showing. It's bright pink.

"You don't belong here, and neither do I," Milo says.

They leave the ballroom and head to a couch in the hotel lobby. The conversation begins. It lasts for more than two weeks. Milo and Ramona can't seem to keep their words off each other. Ramona especially. She is surprised—surprised and pleased—by the intensity of this new whatever-it-is. She enjoys their whatever-we're-doing, although the is-this-or-isn't-it nature sometimes confuses her. She waits for a sign. Then she looks harder. He calls her his "brand-new friend" and she can't help but wonder, *Is that it?* Then she is ashamed of her ungratefulness. Because what she needs more than anything else is, in fact, a brand-new friend.

You wish you could undo your love for him. It's awkward. It's embarrassing. You can't tell anyone about it, because even the fact of it would alter things—perhaps irreparably.

You wonder if he knows. You pray that he doesn't. You want him to read your mind. You send him messages. The telepathy never works.

You try to fall for other people, because maybe he'll like you then.

He tries to set you up with one of his friends. Jim, you're told, is interested in philosophy. Your philosophy, you tell him, is to not be interested in Jim. Because—it's true—Jim blows his nose more often than normal people do. He laughs (his remarkable laugh) and jokes about your ridiculous standards. "There's nothing standard about your standards," he says, and you say that someday your prince will come. More than anything, you want him to reply, "But what if your prince is right under your nose?" Instead he says, "Well, as long as he's not one of those *deposed* princes. . . ."

You wish he'd get a clue. But you're not about to give him one.

You wish he weren't such a prince. You wish he were a frog.

■　■　■

Milo confesses his love to Ramona. (Ramona imagines this as she walks to the subway.) He proclaims, declaims, and just plain claims. He compares his love to oxygen and then describes her in terms of fire. He confesses that she mixes his metaphors and pervades his imagery. He has seen their future written in clouds, transcribed in dreams. His feelings are unanimous, and his friends are, too: He must be with Ramona. He says this—he says it all aloud. Then he turns off the shower and gets ready for dinner. (Note: she does not picture him explicitly in the shower. It's steamy. She can't really see anything.) Ramona will be coming over in twenty minutes.

He, who is rarely befuddled, cannot decide what to wear. (She goes through the options as she boards the train and it moves forward.) He puts on a tie, and figures that's too formal. He puts on a T-shirt, and feels it's not enough. Blue isn't right and red makes his eyes look stoned. He puts on a turtleneck, rolls up the sleeves, puts them back down. He looks at his watch. He makes sure his phone is on, just in case she calls. (Ramona smiles as she steps out of the subway.) He continues to clean the kitchen, happy his parents won't be home for hours. There is a single glass in the sink. He washes it, puts it in the dishwasher, looks at his watch. She is late. His heart feels trepidation. Then he remembers his watch is fast. He checks himself in the mirror again. He switches his shirt, and then changes out of jeans. "Ramona . . . ," he rehearses. He proofreads himself, again in the mirror. He doesn't like the way his mouth looks when he speaks. (She loves his mouth, lingers on it for a second.) He tries to say "Ramona" with his mouth shut. He hears footsteps. He composes himself, opens the door. It is someone he's never seen before, heading to another apartment. (Ramona rings the buzzer.) The buzzer rings. It startles him. His feet lift in the air. No, they just feel like they're lifting in the air.

"Ramona?" he asks as he presses the TALK button. And now LIS-TEN. It is her. (Ramona pictures him expectant.) He closes the dishwasher. He looks at his reflection. He repeats her name. There is so much he has to say. (She knocks. He opens the door.)

Carefully, very carefully, you begin to send signals. You ask her to make most of the decisions, with the hope (but not the expectation) that eventually she will make the right one. You imagine (ha!) that the usual rounds of "I-don't-know-what-do-you-want-to-do?" will end up with her leaning over and kissing you and saying, "There— that's what I want to do."

This does not happen.

Instead, your "signals"—which seem to you to be so obvious and fat, so loud and behemoth—are as remote to her as the shift of an atom. The conversation does not halt—it does not thin itself and be-come a conversion. You falter, fall back to asides, to jokes—she laughs, you are amusing. She doesn't know. You wonder if it's better that way. Enlightenment is scary. Sometimes things look better in the dark.

You could stop her laughter in a second. Force it.

You don't want to.

You back away from an awkward pause.

These are some of the things you cannot say to her:

"When I am with you, there is nowhere else I'd rather be. And I am a person who always wants to be somewhere else."

"I see you in my dreams. And not just in fourth-grade class-rooms or underwater Tupperware parties or other nonsensical dream places. I see you in reality most."

"I'm sorry. I didn't choose this. It just happened."

• • •

Milo is distracted, struck, left without a center of gravity. His shoes don't match, and neither do his socks. He doesn't notice. He lights candles and forgets about them, only to find the wax and ashes the next day. He puts CDs in the washing machine and throws recyclables in the sink. He is haunted by a muffled ringing. (His cell phone is in the laundry basket. It will take him three days to find it.)

Ramona is on her way over. Milo regrets this, because really all he can think about is William.

Two hours ago, he almost said something. To William, not Ramona. He does not say as much as he should to Ramona, and he says even less to William. Or, rather, he says too much to William—everything except those three words, although at least he can use the *I* and the *you* in other contexts. He can avalanche William with words—stories, litanies, tangents, anyways—without letting the biggest boulder loose.

And yet, two hours ago. They were at a gallery, seeing the work of a Japanese photographer who has traveled the world to capture seascaped horizons—the ocean meeting the sky without any land or ship or human in sight. Night and day, calm and storm—gray, black, and white indivisible.

Milo could have looked at the photographs, but he looked at William instead. The glass on the frames was reflective; Milo could see William's eyes move to find the border between sky and sea. Milo saw his own hand moving to William's shoulder—but, no, that was just a daydream mapped on the glass that Milo was placing over reality. They moved from one photo to the next—William covered the placards with his palm and asked Milo to guess the place they were seeing. Milo was invariably wrong—he guessed Cape Horn for the

Carolinas, Alaska for the south of Wales. He even guessed Switzerland. William didn't point out that Switzerland doesn't touch any oceans; Milo realized it himself. "Guess guess guess," William asked, playfully tugging at Milo's sleeve, patting his back tenderly after the third consecutive miss. *Guess guess guess*, Milo thought, patting William likewise, looking at his eyes in the next reflection. When William was quiet again, when he resumed his immersion in the photography and let out a sigh, Milo felt his heart lurch. It was a strange and heretofore unknown feeling—but it felt perfectly natural, as if Milo had nothing to do with it. It was tidal. Milo wanted to tell William about it—which would mean telling William about everything.

But William was already speaking, talking about the length of the exposure and the solitude of the near-daybreak. Milo could not find a transition. He was afraid of souring what had been a wonderful afternoon. William spoke on—of apertures and natural light and the point where the eye is directed. Milo's urgency subsided into a light, bearable sadness.

He tried to look at the pictures.

There comes a moment of decision, if not many. He is talking to you about his morning and suddenly more than anything else you want to kiss him. Or it is night and you are staring at her upturned face, wondering wondering wondering. You share a bed, you share a glance. He changes his shirt in front of you, and you think: *You have no idea how much I love you.* He has no idea. He is the lucky one.

The question is there in each silence. The question is there in the space between you. But you cannot bring it aloud. He is lending you his sweater. She is hugging you hello, and you try to measure for that extra beat. You linger in his apartment, he lingers in your thoughts. When you touch her arm, you feel a charge. You are lying on the floor, watching TV, your legs intertwine with his. You are on the couch laughing. You are breathing in the night sky, lying on your backs. She is pointing out Orion. Your head is on his shoulder, you are riding on the train. You are walking arm in arm through a snowstorm. Singing.

There are good reasons, there are bad reasons—but most of all, there are too many reasons. They cloud, they crush, they deceive. They are too much and never enough.

There is an avoidance in everything. Avoidance, and invention. Ramona rings Milo's doorbell. Milo watches William's mouth as he mentions the still point of morning. Ramona rings the doorbell again. She sits alone in her kitchen. Milo imagines what William would be like as a boyfriend. Ramona invents Milo. Milo invents William. They are all invented.

And you . . . you are not invented. Who do you invent? It goes unspoken.

To love—to fall—is not a question.

To touch—to kiss—to speak—those are questions.

There is nothing worse than a ruined friendship. There is nothing better than a companion. Somewhere in between lies risk.

Somewhere in between, lies.

. . .

Ramona reaches over and pulls Milo toward her. She embraces him, she plunges, she will not let go for a minute. She can do it. Milo and William have a conversation about love and halfway through, Milo interjects: "But, William, you know this is how I feel about you?" He can do it. Milo holds Ramona and treasures her. William is surprised, but not displeased. There are happy endings. There have to be.

You have to believe there are kisses and laughs and risks worth taking. What would you have them do?

Ramona and Milo. Milo and William. Kisses and sighs. Ridiculous Boyfriend #9 and you. Him and she.
   They are inventions. They can do things.
   I can't do the things they do. I can invent.

Ramona reaches over and pulls Milo toward her. (You are right there.) She embraces him, she plunges, she will not let go for a minute. (I want this more than words.) She can do it. (I can't.) Milo and William have a conversation about love and halfway through, Milo interjects: "But, William, you know this is how I feel about you?" (I have daydreams where I see this happening.) He can do it. (I just can't.) Milo holds Ramona and treasures her. William is surprised, but not displeased. There are happy endings. (When I write them.) There have to be. (When I write.)

I want to write my life. I want to be able to write my life.

You are a second away from saying it.

You have no idea how much I love you.

HOW THEY MET

I think my favorite family stories are the stories of how my grand-parents met. To think that these two intersections led to my par-ents, led to me. That my very existence owes thanks to a piano, a jeep, Hunter College, and the U.S. Army. One of the two stories I've been told for as long as I can remember being told stories. The other I recently learned. They amaze me because they prove that a single moment can blossom into almost fifty years of togetherness. They prove that my grandparents were once young and crazy and romantic and yearning. They are finished stories to me now—I knew the ending from the first time I heard them. But at the time . . . well, at the time it must have been something.

My Papa Louis and Grandma Alice's story has to begin with the phrase "It was during the war."

It was during the war. My great-aunt Estelle (my grandfather's sister) and a friend of my grandmother's were going to Hunter College. One day they were comparing notes and discovered that both of their siblings were stationed at Fort Benning, Georgia. They decided to do a little matchmaking. Gladys (my grandfather's other sister) wrote to Lou. Irene (one of my grandmother's sisters) wrote to Alice. Lou got on the horn to Alice. A date was set.

But Lou wasn't going to leave everything to chance. He was thirty-three, a paratrooper. He'd been a cop in New York City before the war and had been on a date or two. He decided to make sure everything was on the up and up before going on a blind date. So a couple of days beforehand he borrowed a jeep and did a drive-by lookover. He found out where my grandmother was going to be and (for lack of a better term) checked her out. He liked what he saw. The date was on.

My grandmother was nine years younger than my grandfather. She was a dietician, and outranked my grandfather. When my grandfather called her up, they arranged to meet Friday for lunch. They hit it off, and my grandmother asked my grandfather if he wanted to go to synagogue with her. This would end up being one of the few times my grandfather would go to temple in his life. (The things we do for love.) He said yes. They met. They talked and talked and talked.

Something clicked.

My grandmother told her friends she'd met this crazy guy. Crazy in a good way.

My grandmother must have been pretty crazy, too. Crazy in a good way.

They were both clearly crazy for each other.

They met on Friday.

By Wednesday they were engaged and talking to a rabbi.

Three days later, after my grandfather's baseball game, they were married.

This is a story we tell all the time. A couple of the details change every now and then, or a character is added (what was the name of the justice who married them?). But the moral of the story is that it worked. They knew, and they were right.

It wasn't until my Pop-Pop Arnold had heart surgery that I realized I didn't know how he and my Grandma Grace had met. I asked my mother and she didn't know, either. She got the story, told it to me, and the next time I saw my grandfather I asked him to tell it again. It's a different kind of story than "during the war." But I love it just as much.

My mother's parents met because they often passed each other in the neighborhood. My grandmother was in a group of girls who would hang out on a certain stoop, chatting. My grandfather was in a group of guys who would walk past on their way to work and say hello. Soon they started talking, group with group, and my grandfather's friend, Sidney Throne, decided to set Arnold and Grace up.

I don't know what their first date was, but I do know that they had such a good time that my grandfather traveled to another borough in order to walk her home. They said good night, saw each other a little more, and eventually it came time for my grandmother to bring my grandfather home.

My great-grandmother was not amused. My grandfather was from Detroit. He'd run away to escape the Ford factory and his parents. He was not from a Fine Jewish Family, like my grandmother was. According to my grandfather, the moment my great-grandmother set eyes on him, she thought, *Who is this shmegegie?*

"She wouldn't give me a glass of water" is how my grandfather tells it. He was ushered into the living room, where all the chairs had cords over them, like antiques in a museum. The only place that didn't have a cord was the piano bench. The piano itself was an ugly green Steinway, never used. My grandfather squeezed in among the clunky furniture, made small talk, but was never offered anything polite, not even a glass of water.

This repeated a few times.

Then one day, sitting on the piano bench, my grandfather decided to open the piano. With my great-grandmother out of the room, he started to play for Grace. He had been to Juilliard, you see, and the room was soon filled with music. My great-grandmother stormed in, disbelieving. Then slowly she went over to the window closest to the piano and opened it. Then the next window. Window after window. So the neighbors could hear. So the neighbors could know what kind of visitor they had.

The next time, he got a glass of water.

Is this the whole story? Of course not, in either case. But these are the true-life family fairy tales, and I'm happy to be the one to tell them ever after.

In 1964, in the summer after they graduated from high school, my parents were set up on a blind date. They went to see *A Hard Day's Night*.

I am here because of a piano, a jeep, Hunter College, the U.S. Army, the Beatles, and a whole bunch of matchmakers. I am here because of letters written during a war, music played with windows open, a crazy leap.

And love. I am here because of love.

MEMORY DANCE

Wallace liked his cornflakes to be served the same way every morning—with only enough milk to surround (and not dampen) the cereal, perhaps with a piece of fruit thrown in. He was accustomed to having them day after day, a constant in his unextraordinary life.

The other constant in Wallace's life, of more importance than the cornflakes, was Mary, who for forty years had sat across the breakfast table from him. Recently, she had been the same every morning, too, dressed in a bowed blouse, blue skirt, and white sneakers (a gift from one of their few grandchildren), the standard outfit for a schoolteacher over sixty.

That day started like many others before it, with Mary waking first and Wallace wandering into the kitchen after ample time was provided to make coffee and pour orange juice (coffee for him and orange juice for her). Wallace had on a bathrobe over his flannel pajamas; he had recently been feeling a chill during the unpredictable April nights.

"Any coffee?" he asked as he entered the kitchen, more out of habit than thirst.

"Here," she answered, pouring the coffee into a World's Greatest Grandmother mug, leaving just enough space at the top for the milk.

The cornflakes box and bowl were already on the table, awaiting Wallace's use. As he sat upon a cushion worn thin over the years, his wife impulsively went to the refrigerator and got Wallace the milk for his cereal. And although she realized that he could have gotten up himself, she always did it. Bringing the milk was merely one of the many constant mini-actions in her life, and to change the process would only make her think about it, thus making the whole thing much more complicated than it was.

"Thank you," Wallace said, always routinely appreciative.

"You're welcome," Mary mumbled, as she walked the ten steps to retrieve her toast from the toaster.

Sitting at the table, neither of them was terribly interested in the other. Granted, had one been missing, the other would have noticed. Yet breakfasts could be eaten with little more than a few words spoken between the lifemates. They had been together so long that superfluous conversation ("Nice weather we're having," "What time did you go to sleep last night?") did not need to be voiced. It was assumed.

That morning, however, the morning was in some manner disrupted. It started very innocently; Mary had been looking at a slightly askew picture frame behind Wallace when he, sensing her head's movement, looked up to match her glance. But when Mary's gaze shifted back from beyond Wallace, she couldn't see him at all. She suddenly found herself reaching through the bonds of time and under the tattered layers of skin.

A hand appeared before her—a man's hand free of age spots and prominent veins. And when she followed the hand to see its keeper, she saw him again, the one she had only seen long ago.

He was a young man once more, looking polite and hesitant, like one of her fourth-grade students on the eve of a school dance. His smile was a mixture of delight and fear, his voice searching to sound assured.

"Would you care to dance?" he said, without a quake and barely a motion.

"Oh, I could hardly . . . ," she said, putting down her wedge of toast.

"Um . . . why not?" said the familiar stranger, starting to sway back and forth, anxiety and doubt starting to make themselves known.

"It's just . . . in this skirt?" she asked, more out of reaction than out of thought. Yet, when she motioned to reinforce her statement, she saw her blue skirt had turned into the bottom of a blue dress. Her white sneakers had disappeared to be replaced by a pair of blue formal shoes. In surprise, she ran her hands down the cotton of the dress and noticed that her fingers looked younger, too.

He paused. Paralyzed with rejection.

"Oh, what am I saying? I'd love to," Mary concluded aloud, going along with the game being played.

She took the hand before her and stood within the kitchen, seeing nothing but her unearthly partner. Slowly, the white tile of her kitchen gave way to the brown, white, and blue of a dance hall. Her appliances disappeared amid a flurry of true metallic music, the triumph of horns and drums that had been nearly forgotten in the distant present.

"I hope you don't mind a slow song," he said, gaining confidence as he led her onto the dance floor.

"Oh, no. I like slow songs. I'm not much of a dancer, never have been, but slow songs just seem easier," she found herself saying effortlessly.

"I think they are, too," he confessed, smiling deeply into her eyes. Gradually, his arms stretched around her, as the band regained its melody.

She gave in at once in his arms, feeling security that she had felt for the first time long ago. Her smile matched his, her soul was his for the taking (she knew now as she didn't know then).

As they danced, the hall faded away. They were light amid a darkened space, with events and faces flashing by.

Their figures drew closer at times and distanced themselves at others, bombarded by emotions and discord somewhat out of their control. Yet, with their eyes meeting and their bodies embraced, the music could not be destroyed. At times the perception of the sound changed, but the song remained the same.

Backward to forward. Forward to backward. They were once again in each other's arms on the dance floor. The music resumed its earthly tone, letting that moment's dance slide gracefully to a halt, joined by applause of appreciation for the music's makers.

For a moment, the couple remained embraced. Her cheeks dimpled with a smile. His eyes moved over her shoulder.

Slowly, his hands lowered.

"It's a shame that's the last song," she said, seeing the finality in his eyes as he looked at the clock.

"There'll be more tomorrow," he said, with yet another grin. "Do you think I could see you then?"

"Certainly," she said, walking with him toward the door.

"Until then," he remarked upon departure, walking into the balmy summer night, his thoughts and hopes as incomplete as his farewell.

As he left, she sat herself down, seeing the decorations undone around her. In her lap was a clean handkerchief someone had left on the chair next to hers.

Before her eyes, the handkerchief slowly transformed, as Mary returned to the familiar. It metamorphosized from cotton to silk to velvet to paper, from white to red to blue to yellow, until all that was left was a napkin in her lap.

Mary quickly glanced to her side, seeing the kitchen once more. Although nothing in the room had changed, she felt that some things did not seem to be the way they had been before. She centered her sight and saw Wallace again. Looking into his steady eyes, she had a feeling that he felt it, too. The music had faded, but it was there all the same, awaiting the next crescendo.

INTERSECTION

It takes a thousand people to create an accident. The man who installed the traffic sign a little askew. The woman who held the elevator for an extra moment as the driver left his office. The driver's great-grandmother, who fell in love with the man at the hat shop. The driver's two-thirty appointment, who had to put him on hold because of another call (his ten-year-old daughter). The technician who made the song on the radio sound so good. The television weatherman who had predicted rain.

Person after person after person . . . they all converge at one moment, irrevocably changing the course of a thousand more lives.

As it is with accidents, so it is with love.

Meredith and John are standing in the Elysian Fields, on the edge of Hoboken, overlooking the New York City skyline. The sky is so dark that all the lights are magical. It is late in the hour, late in the night, late in the year. And yet the air is filled with beginnings—sweet, giddy lightness and the languid feel of clocks at rest.

John and Meredith dance. They dance to the sound of the fabric-maker who made John's sleeve so soft. They dance to the sound of their families' arguments, and to the sound of their grandparents' praise. They dance to the sounds that are carried in the airwaves around them—radio transmissions at lunar speed, one of which carries Meredith's favorite song from high school, bound for another listener, miles away.

They dance to the sound of a baby's heartbeat. They dance to the sound of their first kiss.

Somewhere back in time, a boy named Daryl broke Meredith's heart. Somewhere back in time, John woke up driving at night, and swerved just in time to miss a tree. Somewhere back in time, Meredith's parents said *I love you*. Somewhere back in time, a man said, *This land should be a park*. Another man's wife named it Elysian Fields.

Right now, a man in a red Chevrolet is driving by. Right now, John's boss is getting ready for bed—her husband rolls over and gives her a corner of his pillow. Right now, the friend who taught Meredith to kiss in fourth grade is thinking about her, wondering where she is.

Every two people cause an intersection.

Every person alters the world.

Meredith's grandparents were married so long that their time together acquired all the time before and all the time after, so it could be truly said that they are married forever. John's parents are much the same way.

At any given moment, there are millions of people saying their lover's name. The words travel through the air.

Meredith leans into John, her hand loosely on his sleeve. He pushes a stray hair behind her ear and leaves his palm on her cheek. Then he retreats, and moves closer. The lights of Manhattan twinkle.

They kiss.

Maybe fate's arithmetic is so diffuse that it's not arithmetic at all.

The lights. The sleeve. The park. The taxpayers of Hoboken. The parents. The friends. The past. The swaying of the streetlights. The car passing. The present. The hopes. The break-ups. The conversations. The invention of the lightbulb.

It is the miracle of all these things coming together that constitutes love. The orchestra has been assembled . . . and now it plays.

It doesn't have to be on Valentine's Day. It doesn't have to be by the time you turn eighteen or thirty-three or fifty-nine. It doesn't have to conform to whatever is usual. It doesn't have to be kismet at once, or rhapsody by the third date.

It just has to be. In time. In place. In spirit.

It just has to be.

Two people in a park—

They kiss.

An intersection.